In *The Rhythm of the Soul* Lisa D. McCall has accomplished an amazing feat. Weaving beautiful prose with a poetic grace, she bridges cultures and paradigms to reveal what is most essential in life – retrieving, healing and recovering our soul. In this powerful journey, Laila is caught between two worlds: modern and ancient, east and west, old and new. As she struggles with her father wound, we begin to see our own wounds of patriarchal culture woven in her story. I found myself moved to tears as this brave young woman learns to give up what she thought she knew so she can discover what the desert and the Tuareg people mirror about her own heart; and that is in letting go of everything, she can find belonging in the vast emptiness of just being.

There are so many gems of wisdom and moving quotes that cut to the core of what life is about, and how the desert forever teaches by taking away. Being the father of an only daughter, I found it personally meaningful to have a story of a brave female protagonist finding herself in a world that too often teaches women to play small and deny their own hearts and truth. I highly recommend this book as a journey of self-discovery and a regaining of the dark feminine wisdom that lies within our own hearts and helps us discover our full belonging in the great mystery of just being!

~ Michael Brant DeMaria, Ph.D., Psychologist, bestselling author and 4-time Grammy nominee

Lisa D. McCall's *The Rhythm of the Soul* invites us into the magical, devastating, ineffable beauty of both the Sahara desert and our own inner landscapes. The story's protagonist, Laila returns to the Tuareg guides she had known as a child, carrying with her a tragic past and a current yearning "for an outer landscape large enough to allow her to fall into the void of her heart." Inspired by her own quests into the depths of the Sahara, Lisa's narrative dissolves the conventional boundaries of family, culture and possibility and shows us how to live "around, among and between" them.

> ~ Reggie Marra, author of *And Now, Still* and *The Quality of Effort*

*The Rhythm of the Soul* takes us on a journey with the Tuareg nomads of the Sahara Desert. Lisa D. McCall weaves their story into her fictional novel with much respect and mindfulness. Through her imaginative style of moving between voices and narrators, their culture and complex history comes alive. Exploring these topics and the reflexivity needed to do it well is not easy, but Lisa pulls it off. She transports you into another world without stepping into the pitfalls that can befall writing about people so culturally different. There is a rhythm to the book that is lovely. I really enjoyed reading this work!

> ~ Rory Turner, Ph.D., Assistant Professor, Sociology and Anthropology, Goucher College, Towson, MD.

# The Rhythm of the Soul

# A Journey of Loss and Discovery

## LISA DIANE MCCALL

Copyright © 2016 Lisa Diane McCall

All rights reserved.

ISBN-13: 978-0692889374

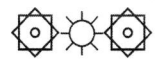

I dedicate this story to my family and friends who have been part
of my life's journey to create it.

With your love and support, I have been able to
fully live, as well as write
the rhythm of my soul.

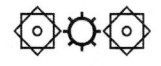

# CONTENTS

| | |
|---|---|
| Acknowledgments | i |
| Foreword | iii |
| An Interstitial Connection | 7 |
| Rite of Passage: Stage I, Severance | 9 |
| Rite of Passage: Stage II, Threshold | 72 |
| Rite of Passage: Stage III, Incorporation | 129 |

# ACKNOWLEDGMENTS

First I must thank Sabina Wyss and Marianne Roth* from Switzerland. For many years they traveled to the Sahara Desert forging deep connections and trust with the Tuaregs. Guiding vision quests in the Sahara Desert through their organization, Kamelkarawanen, along with the Tuareg who took care of us, offered a journey unlike any others I know. Given the relationships they built with the Tuaregs, we were able to connect with them within days, make that hours, of our journey. In only a two to three week period, our lives intertwined as we walked and rode camels, drank shai tea, ate meals out of the same bowls, laughed, and shared tales about our disparate cultures. We got the chance to combine deep inner work in the midst of an anthropological experience. Special thanks to Adem Mellakh, our lead Tuareg, who organized the caravan and to Jumbo who was our medicine man on the 2005 quest.

Much gratitude goes to Trebbe Johnson. She is the key person who informed me about the Sahara vision quest. She was also my guide along with Sabina on both of my quests. Trebbe has supported me not only in the Sahara, but over many years with her wise, intense mirroring and guidance. She continuously fed my inspiration to write this story and delivered me to my writing coach, Jennifer Wilhoit.

Thanks to all my family and friends for their encouraging feedback as I read passages to them over the years. Although writing a book encompasses much alone time, community is so important for sharing and to keep you sane. Thanks to my co-questers from my second Sahara vision quest. We bonded as a "desert family" so we are able to keep that shared experience alive. Special appreciation to Oliver Scheuvens for helping me with Tamasheq words and to Malu Lalla Deck for sharing her experiences in a Tuareg village on a return journey.

Deepest gratitude goes to Jennifer Wilhoit, Ph.D., writing coach extraordinaire. When we met, my writing practice was as dried up as the desert. Jennifer offered support in much more than writing. My mother had just died before we met. Jennifer's intuitive way guided me through my grief, not only about my mother's passing, but the grief of losing touch with my story. She brought parts of me back to life, reawakened my awareness, and fed me with love and acceptance. I expanded from her care which fed the words I wrote. I would never have gotten this book completed without her.

Thanks to Trebbe Johnson, Reggie Marra, Dr. Michael Brant DeMaria, and Dr. Rory Turner for taking time in their busy schedules to read my manuscript and providing their enthusiastic reviews. Also to Reggie who guided me into and held my hand through the self-publishing process.

And although I have had mixed feelings about having to exist in this world, I want to thank my parents, Olivia and Dave, for the "oops" that became me. And to my siblings who are the best ever, Richard, Stephen, and Susan. How fortunate I am to have been dropped into this family to feel your support and love.

---

*Tragically Marianne died in a car accident in the Sahara the year before my first trip. She and Adem were married.

# FOREWORD

This story is a tale based upon stepping into the unknown and perseverance, without which it would never have been written.

In 2003, there came an opportunity that called deeply to me – a vision quest into the Sahara Desert on caravan with camels and the Tuareg nomads. Thinking about this journey made my fingers tingle with excitement along with hearing a resounding inner "YES!" that I must go. Where that urge came from, I still to this day do not know, but the unknown called and I heeded. The lure of the never ending sand and stars, blue sky, exotic nomads, and dragon like camels stirred my heart and soul, not to mention my imagination, with an intensity I could not ignore. (There was also the influence of *Lawrence of Arabia*, one of my favorite movies.)

When I finally arrived in Southern Algeria in January 2005 and began the trek into the vastness of the Sahara, a region I had never thought about at any other time in my life, I was struck by how familiar the foreign landscape felt to me. A sense of the unknown known, but filled with mysteries longing to be discovered. Those discoveries were rich and deep and, I figured, I could be content having had that experience of a lifetime. But, no... exploring the unknown was not yet complete.

Because a few years later, without warning, without any hint or preview, another longing to go back arose. This time with an intensity that rivaled the first inner "YES!" I wasn't sure why, but I heeded the call of the unknown again and returned to the Sahara in January 2010. Nestled between that longing and my return trip, this story began to reveal itself.

The longing to write was another unknown in my life. Although I had had the habit of journaling for many years, I felt the urge to write fictional stories a few years before my first Sahara calling. I attended a variety of writing classes, in which one of the teachers used a phrase that resonated with me – the unthought known – and so I heeded that exploration.

I began penning *The Rhythm of the Soul* in late 2008. (Although the title did not come to me until after I finished the story.) It began bubbling up to my mind's eye as if I was viewing scenes from a movie. I wrote down what I saw. I then decided to take the passages I had written thus far with me on the second vision quest and read them to my guides and co-questers. As we sat in the desert, sharing our life stories, I also shared the life of my fictional story. The feedback I received was more than positive, which I thought would spur my writing on to completion perhaps by the end of 2010. But, alas, this is where perseverance entered.

When I returned from that (even more incredible) quest, I thought my writing muse would feel indulged by all the inspiration and experiences. It did for a while, but I found something out about the book writing process – it is anything but easy. Sometimes sparks of inspiration burn and other times they fizzle out. Sometimes the relationship with your words and the story feel like a honeymoon all cozy and intimate, but sometimes they seem to turn on a dime and divorce you. Like any loving relationship, there must be perseverance to rekindle the spark of love. It's a process of figuring out how to keep falling in love over and over again. I was in a spotty relationship, which ultimately went fallow. I even tried using a writing app to help. It quickly became more about understanding how to navigate the app than the actual writing itself. The story became lost in app-ville and it didn't reappear for years.

I tried to forget it. I tried to shove the possibility of ever finishing it away. I thought that I had at least given it a good try. Some people finish writing books, well, I just wasn't one of them. But a sensation deep inside kept niggling at me. It wouldn't go away whatever I did to distract myself. It always made itself known, but when it went from low grade niggling to outright discomfort, that is when I had to take a drastic step – one that many couples take when they try to rescue their relationships. I had to bring in a third party, an objective counselor. In my case, it was a writing coach.

Through her deftly crafted coaxing, she enabled me to pick up the pen again. I extracted my story from the black chasm of that writing app and she fed my perseverance to somehow get to the end of the story. Even with my computer crashing and losing a part I was writing along the way, she kept me inspired, accountable, and on task.

So here is my offering that came from living the unknown, writing the unthought, and the perseverance to find creative ways not to give up. May you delve where you least expect to go and seek what niggles within you.

By the way, what are the unknowns that niggle within you? And more importantly, will you persevere to explore them?

Lisa Diane McCall, 2017

"The desert is the only cure for despair. Because the desert is an infinite space, the silence of the dunes, a night sky enameled with a thousand stars. Here are surroundings which unfailingly save even the most desperate. In the desert, one can weep without worrying about flooding a riverbed. No landscape is more propitious to meditation. It was for this that every great prophet was born in the desert."
*Ahmadou Kourouma*

## AN INTERSTITIAL CONNECTION

The strains of a guitar penetrate a pitch-black sky jeweled with brilliant stars. Four men, veiled so that only their eyes are revealed between yards of fabric wrapped 'round and 'round their heads, sit near a fire. These are the Tuareg nomads, the so-called Blue Men of the Sahara Desert. They are resting from a long day's trek with their caravan, drinking their shai tea in a remote area of the Ahaggar Mountains; it's so isolated that only celestial bodies, be they God, *djinn* spirits, or orbiting satellites, know that they are there.

Gazing at the glowing flicker of the flames, the Tuareg know they are not alone. Their pensive eyes, floating within the frame of so many layers of cotton, watch forms appear and disappear in the smoke. Years of experience penetrating into the deepest parts of the Ahaggar Mountains provided numerous accounts of inexplicable occurrences. Deep in the Sahara, *djinni* dance across the thresholds of time and space with abandoned delight, toying with the human world.

As the music comes to an end, one of the Tuareg, Go'at, speaks. "*Inshallah*, (God willing), a visitor will be here in two days. A girl, now woman, is making her way back after twenty years away. She lives a life deeply touched by our land and people. Her family studied our ways and our language. She is journeying to where her father and my good friend, Jack, was killed." Go'at rearranges the logs of the dying fire with a stick.

"We will guide her through this land, her heart, and the visions of our tea ritual. It is up to God if and when she enters visions from the three rounds of the shai tea we brew: bitter like life, strong like love, and sweet like death. It will be our honor to hold a sacred space for her journey." Go'at shifts his focus to one of the men and addresses him.

"Ouhetta."

"*Ayouen*," the typical response in Tamasheq, the language of the Tuareg.

Go'at continues, "You must be sure that your camel, Anarani, is with us. It has been many caravans since he carried the girl, Laila, and her father. Laila bonded with Anarani and I want him to carry her again. He may provide some comfort as she uncovers the yearnings she feels deep within this desert and her heart."

Beyond their small circle lies a silence so dark and vast, it encompasses the restlessness of the world. And soon a woman whose heart feels that discontent will be entering the void of sand, sky, and her own longings. Quietly the men sit. The fire's searing breathiness hisses. Sparks rise up like fingers coiling around the velvety void, reaching out to a room thousands of miles away…

※

…and in her bedroom, Laila performs her morning ritual of lighting a candle in memory of her father who never returned from the Sahara Desert twenty years ago. His ashes remained behind as she and her mother made their way back to the States steeped in grief. The flame flickers wildly, though no windows are open. She stares at the fluttering candle, contemplating her trip back to the desert she last knew as a child.

For a brief moment, Laila discerns a hint of a figure rising from the tip of the bouncing flame. There is something enigmatic and hypnotizing about the movement. She is mesmerized. The agitated flame reflects how much is stirring within her heart. Trepidation mixes with excitement in these days before traveling back to where she last saw her father, the Tuareg, and the wide, open desert that used to be her home.

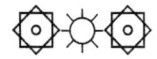

# RITE OF PASSAGE: STAGE I
# SEVERANCE

(Hearing the call, preparing to leave, entering into the unknown)

## LAILA'S JOURNAL ENTRY

It is only a few days before my flights will deliver me once again into the expansive space of the Sahara Desert. This morning I already found myself there in a dream. I am standing at the threshold of a mighty sandstorm, on the verge of being swallowed up. My father is running toward me so he can protect me. The closer the sandstorm approaches, the faster time races by, while the distance of my father gets farther and farther away. Just as the hazy edge of its driving force reaches me, I wake up with a start. The feeling of time and my heart racing lingers over my semiconscious state. Then in an instant, awareness takes hold and my mind begins running through all the errands to be done for this trip.

Although all the arrangements are set for my arrival in Tamanrasset, I am still preparing myself emotionally for what will come. But, of course, how does one prepare to walk into a threshold of unknowns? My sleep has been restless between dreams and waking up. I have been waking up at least once during these nights. I feel a tingling sensation in the pit of my stomach. I don't think it is only about being scared. It feels like something deeper than that and I can only describe it as a vibrating longing to break free and come alive.

I have been taking walks in the woods to contemplate my feelings and the restlessness deep in the core of my being. It helps me sort through the voices swirling around and inside of my head. And when I finally find space amidst the din, I hear a message bubbling up about feeling vulnerable. I realize the tingling of fear is letting me know that I must let go of my layers of protection. I must allow myself to be vulnerable, but how?

Like the Tuareg who traditionally wore swords for personal protection as well as to protect the goods of their caravans, I decided to find an object that would symbolically provide protection in my journey. The first thing that came to mind was a Tuareg amulet to ward off bad spirits, a gift that my father gave me just before he died. I will wear it to feel his presence with me. In the process of finding the amulet, I came across a little silver Tuareg cup that was made for me when I was born. Oh, and I will take my origami paper since I love making peace cranes. I feel like it may be a way to connect with people, especially children. Although I am trying to scale back the contents of my baggage, these items call out to be taken, and so I shall.

## THE TUAREG

"The way of the nomad may be dispersed, one journey here, another there, but our footsteps have always been rooted in the soul of the Sahara. Over many years, we have been subject to forces that expect us to assemble like those who dwell in the city, to give up our deep relationship with the sand, sky, water, and air. We have seen the city and for us Tuareg it's lonelier than the vast desert. We may not be assembled like those in the city but we still have a strong sense of place. Place is crucial to belonging. Through our stories and tea ceremony, we will guide Laila to not only find her place in the Sahara, but also into the rooted belonging of her soul."

## A PATH LESS KNOWN

When her departure day finally came, Laila was proud that she kept the volume of her belongings to only one large and one small backpack. She knew they would be strapped to the pack camels, so she wanted to minimize their burden. Besides, there were not many clothes she had to pack due to the fact that she would be wearing the traditional garb of the Tuareg men: a *shesh*–yards of fabric wrapped like a turban around her head, and a *gandora*–a tunic with matching, loose fitting pants.

Laila waited for the cab's arrival to take her to the airport. She had said her farewell to her mother the prior evening. It was hard enough for her mother to see her daughter going back to the desert, so she did not want to go to the airport for her goodbyes. Laila checked everything – passport, visa for Algeria, flight itinerary, and her backpacks. Just at that moment, she heard a beep and saw the driver getting out of the cab. Her stomach fluttered with butterflies.

Riding in the cab, she couldn't believe her venture, her quest, was about to begin. But then again, she thought, when did it really begin? She saw an image in her mind of the last time she had been in the desert. It was of a ceremony held for the death of her father twenty years ago. She was still a child. Laila remembered holding her mother's hand and the hand of a Tuareg girl who was older than her. It was a long time since she let herself conjure up that memory. Any memories from that time had been safely tucked away, but they must have wanted to be released. That part of her had been buried for too long and she couldn't ignore it anymore. Her soul's call from deep within was louder than ever. As much as it brought up fear, Laila was glad that she decided to finally pay attention to follow the path less known.

## THE CALL OF THE DESERT

Exhausted from the flights, not to mention the logistics of getting through the Algiers and Tamanrasset airports, Laila sat on the bed in a sparsely decorated room of a lodge on the outskirts of Tamanrasset. The only item that held any visual interest was the multi-striped camel blanket beneath her. She welcomed the simplicity of the room and the desert environs. This lodge was where her parents used to stay before launching into and returning from the Ahaggar Mountains and the surrounding desert of southern Algeria for their field studies with the Tuareg. She got up to look out the small, shuttered window; the compound sat on reddish dirt and had a white building housing the common toilets and showers, encircled by adobe rooms. The last time she had been here she was a child with her mother. They were both dealing with the tragic circumstance that had altered their lives.

❁☼❁

Laila's parents began their studies in the mid 1980's and concentrated mostly on the nomads of southern Algeria. Her parents' area of focus was the Tuareg culture. These nomads of the Sahara Desert are also called the "Blue Men" for the indigo dye that colors the fabric of their turban or *shesh*, and rubs off on their skin giving it a bluish hue. As typical anthropologists, Laila's parents lived with the Tuareg as participant-observer researchers, learning the customs and language of the tribes over many years.

Katherine stayed stateside while Laila was a baby. Jack tried to fly home as much as he could during that time. When Laila reached school age, Katherine and Jack decided to let the desert and their experiences lay a foundation for her teachings. Her parents schooled Laila in all the expected topics and more as she soaked up this nomadic culture. As an only child of anthropologist parents, Laila lived a life other children would only read about in books; a life that might be perceived as foreign to Westerners became for

Laila simply the way the world was.

In the early 1990's, Tuareg resentment toward the government, competition for scarce resources, and distrust of non-Tuareg farmers created an atmosphere of conflict that eventually grew into a revolution. Much of the conflict was located in northern Niger and Mali, but there was unrest among factions in southern Algeria as well. This area had not experienced as much violence, but men were armed and had trained at revolutionary camps in Mali and Libya.

The family remained during the build-up of this resistance, but it became increasingly dangerous. They knew they must leave, especially for Laila's sake. Unfortunately, the consequences of the revolution touched the family deeply. While saying their goodbyes in a village near the Algeria and Niger border, a skirmish broke out with gunfire in the unsuspecting village, turning an ordinary moment of daily life into chaos. As people ran for cover, Jack was shot in his attempt to find a safe cover for his family. It did not kill him instantly, but by the time his key informant Go'at found him, he was nearing his last breath. Heartbroken and devastated, Laila and her mother never returned to the Sahara after losing their beloved.

❁✦❁

Laila stood gazing out at this place that had once felt like home, but now held little familiarity for her as an adult. Twenty years of not living in or returning to the Sahara, coupled with a lack of desire to even listen to news about the Tuareg, diminished her connection. Yet, childhood experiences have deep and lasting effects. Stepping back into the setting that influenced her throughout her formative years, Laila wondered how many memories would be triggered.

With a weary sigh, she went over to her backpack to pull out some of her things. Regardless of the long journey from the States and as exhausted as she felt, Laila was anxious to get out into the Saharan air. She reached for her journal and decided to find a set of steps that she remembered having fun running up and down as a child. Placing a hat on her head, for even a late afternoon sun in January pours down with a burning intensity, Laila went out on her search. She stood for a second to get oriented outside her door and chuckled, for just to her left were the steps. They were nestled between the rooms and went up to the flat roof. Her travel-weary eyes had not noticed them. She had only been focused on getting settled in her room when she arrived. Now a renewed energy was expanding her vision.

With the enthusiasm of a child, Laila ran up. She gasped at the breathtaking view that opened visual and emotional floodgates, not only to the flowing expanse of the dry desert sand as far as her eyes could see, but also a flashback to hearing her father calling for her to come down for their evening meal. Laila's eyes moistened. She dropped to her knees and buried her face in her hands, crying with a lament that she hadn't known for years.

## THE DESERT

*"God has created a country full of water so that people
can live in it.
But the desert he has created so people
can find their soul in it."
Tuareg proverb*

"I, the largest desert in the world, test the strength of visitors and inhabitants alike allowing no forgiveness. Those who survive my conditions never again live on as the people they were. Over the centuries, many adventurers came to seek their fortunes in gold or to navigate large distances of my terrain not yet traversed by outsiders. My wide expanse beckoned to be conquered, while I laid in wait to swallow up any who dared venture in, especially those arrogant enough to think they could outsmart my harsh and unfamiliar nature. Their tales, if they lived to tell them, inevitably described the horrors of sickness, starvation, dehydration. Some were even attacked and left for dead by the very nomads who had been paid to lead their caravans. They took their last breath on my sandy bed, never again to return to their homeland or loved ones. As a Tuareg saying goes, 'The desert rules you; you do not rule the desert.'

"Yes, those who are drawn into the belly of my existence will feel their despair and discontent surrounded by infinite space, silence, and emptiness. Take my wild nature in with respect and reverence and I am a reminder from God of the vast void all humans feel within. I am an invitation to meditation, a stirring deep in one's soul."

## THE JOURNEY BEGINS

As one penetrates the Sahara Desert's interior, the sheer volume of sand obliterates paved roadways. Attempts at laying highways have been futile for, like any other desert surface, they would disappear, eventually swallowed up by the innumerable grains of drifting sand. Roads, or "pistes," are only distinguishable by parallel and crisscrossing tire tracks in the sand. Scattered over these tracks are camel footprints and their dung. Ancient and modern ways are woven together while neither has taken precedence over the other. Laila forgot how rough and tumble a ride over the desert terrain could be. All the jostling and swerving was a welcome distraction to her busy mind.

Only those most knowledgeable about the myriad sand conditions should attempt to drive the desert pistes. Drivers need two skills to navigate through or around treacherous patches: a keen eye to judge how loose or solid the surface is, and split-second decision-making. The density and texture of the sand dictates the velocity of the vehicle. The softer the sand, the faster the vehicle must be driven so as to keep the tires from sinking in. Of course, completely avoiding this type of stratum is optimal. Laila could tell by the determined look on the driver's face, his eyes staring straight ahead, that she was in capable hands. Besides, he was Tuareg. She knew never to put her trust for desert travel in any other hands.

Heading out from Tamanrasset to the area where she would meet with Go'at, his team, and their camels, Laila's thoughts were scattered. Her mind drifted back to a conversation with her mother that delivered her to this distant journey.

※ ※ ※

Laila and her mother were finishing dinner one evening. Katherine thought their exchange during the meal had not been as animated as usual.

"Honey, what's wrong?" Katherine asked, sensing that her daughter's mind was weighing her down. "And don't give me that, 'nothing' glazed over response because I know better."

"Nothing," she still responded with an upbeat tone as she was drying the dishes her mother was washing after dinner.

Her mother gave her the look that had always induced

confessions since she was a little girl. "Okay, okay. I have been thinking."

"Thinking about what?"

"I've been thinking a lot lately about Dad and the Sahara and my life and ... and ... I don't know. Something inside of me just doesn't seem right. I feel like there's something I can't get to or understand about myself, about how things are. It was so hard coming back without Dad. Even though we tried to settle in and get back to normal, there was never any normal again."

"Laila," her mom turned to her and led her to the kitchen table to sit down. "Laila, I know that nothing about our lives, and especially your upbringing, had any semblance to others' experiences. You've been grappling with this for a long time. So I'm all ears. Tell me more about what you're struggling with."

Laila sighed. "Don't get me wrong. My childhood was awesome getting to grow up in the Sahara with you and Dad. I wouldn't have had it any other way. It's been such a long time since we left, but the sadness lingers. Something feels unresolved. I can't explain it. I actually let myself watch a documentary about the Tuareg a few weeks ago. I couldn't believe it. I felt this overwhelmingly deep connection bubble up, like I was there only yesterday. And then, well, then I started sobbing. All those memories flooded back. It was amazing to live in that world growing up. I still remember Anarani, the camel. I loved him so much. But after we returned to the States, I knew you didn't want to talk much about being there since the revolution was still going on and, well, what happened to Dad. I'm sorry to be bringing all of this up, Mom."

Katherine ran a motherly hand over he daughter's hair and raised her chin to look into her eyes. "What are you trying to say, Dear?"

"Well, you know how I like to take walks in the woods to, you know, connect with Dad."

Katherine nodded.

"So after seeing that documentary, I thought maybe I would go for a walk and ask for a sign. Something that would help me figure out what to do next. This may sound crazy, but I feel like I heard a voice from someplace deep inside me say, 'Go back.' I just can't shake that voice. It continues to haunt me. So... I feel like I need to return."

"Return... you mean back to the Sahara?"

"Yeah. When I was walking, the words just came out of nowhere. At first I was hearing the phrase 'I should be happy' playing in my mind. I have a good job. I'm independent and comfortable. Yet it feels like there's something more to life. And when have I ever had a relationship that lasted more than a few months or barely a year? There's this empty feeling, a void I can't seem to fill."

Katherine couldn't disagree with her daughter. Those words rang true for her as well. "And what do you think going back to the Sahara will do besides drudge up old memories?" She had secretly feared this day might come and, as any mother would, she also feared the dangers. She wanted to support her daughter. But that meant letting her go to a place that was far away, that was still dealing with rebel activity, repercussions from the revolution they had fled.

"Mom, honestly, this longing to return puzzles the hell out of me, too. I know the last thing you want is to worry about me being someplace that's so remote and with lingering unrest."

Hearing her daughter echo the very sentiment in her head, Laila's mother couldn't help expressing her fearful emotions. "Laila, you took the words right out of my mouth! There are militant factions of Tuareg roaming the desert. You'll be out in the midst of... who knows what. I can't have you do that!" She got up from the table, shaking.

"Mom, Mom," Laila got up to put her arms around Katherine. "Mom, listen to me. I knew you might be upset..."

"Laila," her tone shifted to a worried anger, "we have already dealt with a loss deeper than my heart has been able to handle!" She paused with anxious breathing. Then as she looked at her daughter, she sank back into the sadness. "But you... over there... me not knowing..." She trailed off with tears streaming down her cheeks.

"What if I told you that it feels like Dad is calling me to go back?" With those words, Katherine burst into tears. Laila held her mother and felt the tears welling up in her eyes. "Mom, I'm so sorry! I can't really explain it. But there's this urge deep inside of me that won't stop," she said while comforting her mother.

Laila handed her mom a tissue from the counter. Katherine gathered up her emotions, wiping her tears and blowing her nose.

"Laila, my dear Laila," Katherine sighed. "What circumstances life has handed you!" They looked at each other. A slight smile appeared on their lips, reflecting what only the two of them had shared in life. Her mother broke the pregnant pause saying, "You know I will support you no matter what. So, I hate to ask: what's your plan?"

"I don't exactly know at the moment. But, do you have any suggestions on how I might get in touch with Go'at?"

❁❁❁

Tracking him down was not easy. But her mother pursued old connections and was fortunate to make contact with Go'at. Through him, Laila made arrangements and sent payments to assemble a caravan with nomads, camels, and food. She also sent her size specifications and money for three *gandoras*, so a seamstress could make them along with *sheshes* to wear; her Western clothes would not serve well, culturally or physically, in the desert. In her discussions with Go'at, they decided that she would order the garb traditionally worn by men not women. He suggested that this would make travel in the desert and a caravan easier. Although a caravan is a man's world, they came to the conclusion that being a Western woman allowed her to operate outside the dictates of gender.

Laila worked through months of preparation for this trip. Then the long flights from country to country and city to city finally brought her to the Sahara once again. As she penetrated deeper into the desert, distant memories began to flood up from her past. It was sinking in that her journey was beginning. Staring from the Land Rover's shaking interior to the outer stillness—composed of a wide, flat valley and surrounding massifs of high, rocky plateaus along with the heaping rock piles below them—her gut stirred. The joy of returning jostled against her apprehension about what she was seeking.

Laila was once familiar with this landscape and now, so many years later, her perception had altered. As a child under the protective watchfulness of her parents and the communities they worked in, she remembered possessing boldness in her corner of the Sahara. Now it was time for her to forge her own path, this time with an adult's awareness of the immense and truly foreign landscape of her surroundings. She was at least walking into nomadic communities once studied by her parents, so she would not be a complete stranger.

Laila had not seen Go'at since she was last in the desert. Since that time, her head had become lined with memories, some vividly underscored but most buried in a misty haze over the natural course of time and distance, and further obscured from the grief of losing her father. Just then, the Land Rover slowed as it made its approach to the area with the camels. Laila was delighted to see Go'at talking in a group.

His head was wrapped in the *shesh*. His face with chiseled Arabic features, was completely exposed. It was rare to find men who consistently followed the Tuareg tradition of keeping their face veiled at all times. Laila saw the same face she remembered, save perhaps deeper wrinkles around his eyes when he smiled and laughed, which he did quite often. Go'at's nature lent itself to being irreverently compassionate, humorously pointing out the ironies of human behavior or life in a way that never held judgment.

Laila was happy to get out of the vehicle as much to see Go'at as to relieve her cramped legs and rattled body. Go'at looked her way and doubled the glance for this was not the Laila his eyes had last recognized. He left the group and made his way toward her.

"Little Laila?" he called out.

"Yes, Go'at!" Laila exclaimed. Her arms extended as she ran his direction. They embraced, laughing. Go'at stepped back to take in this girl who was all grown up. She might be a woman standing before him, but he could still sense the energy of the girl he remembered.

"Little Laila is not so little anymore," he said, his brows furled as he cocked his head to the side. She lowered her head slightly looking at him from the top of her eyes, a smirk on her lips. Go'at observed how she had grown tall, like her father, and her features were quite strikingly like his as well. Most striking to Go'at, however, was seeing the kindness embedded in her features. If kindness is an inherited trait, she had come by it honestly.

"You are your father's daughter," he commented quietly.

Laila smiled as their eyes exchanged the sadness of their loss, but the moment's excitement could not be contained and tumbled back onto their faces. Laila's smile brightened again.

"It's so good to see you, Go'at! I have missed this part of the world. Tell me everything! Your life, your family, the desert!" Go'at's smile and spirited demeanor diminished a bit. Of what he and the Tuareg had gone through these past years, there was much to tell. But this was not the time.

"I have been fine, fine, but enough talk for the moment. We will have many sunrises to tell the stories we have lived. Come. Let us first find you a camel."

"A camel?" she questioned with an emphasis on the A. "Don't you mean Anarani? Oh, Go'at please tell me he's here with you! You said on the phone that he would be going with us." Go'at heard the tinge of panic in her voice.

"Anarani? Of course, my dear Little, uh, Laila." He paused thinking better of that description of her now. "Yes, Anarani is waiting for you," he responded giving her a wink.

They walked toward the camels gathered below a low canyon wall. The men were preparing for the caravan. They would be heading out the next morning. Along with checking the supplies and equipment, much of their preparation revolved around the camels' well-being. It is important for the Tuareg to check for signs of distress, whether internal or external, since the overall pace moves only as fast as the slowest camel.

"How is your mother?" Go'at asked.

"Truthfully, I don't think she ever completely recovered from the loss of my father. I think a part of her died that day in the village. She regained some of her vitality, but her happiness drained away. She mainly focused on raising me, and teaching. Occasionally, she was able to talk about when we lived here. We even practiced speaking French and Tamasheq with each other. The anthropologist in her didn't want my desert education to be lost." Laila stopped for a moment to summon a sentence for Go'at. *"Maigan dgh Imnäs?"*

Go'at folded his arms, while placing his right hand in front of his lips and chuckled. "Yes, yes, the camels are doing well," he replied. "But you must know that the tragedy with your father hit us very hard as well. Your family has been missed. Many people will be happy to see you." His sentiment helped to reassure her.

When they reached the area with the camels, Go'at told Laila to wait and he would bring Anarani to her. She scanned the herd. She wasn't sure if, after all this time, she could recognize him, but it didn't take long before she felt sure she had picked him out.

Anarani had distinctive scars on his cheeks and his fur was not as thick in those areas. As a child, she had always wondered why he had those scars. When she asked about them, she was told that it was from fighting with another camel, but his nature did not seem to lend itself to such behavior. She remembered that when he was couched, she would rub his cheeks and ears. It seemed to make him happy and she loved how his head gradually lowered until his chin rested on the ground.

Go'at, indeed, went to the camel that Laila had recognized and brought him over to her. He was a slightly smaller camel than some of the others, but his stature was quite high nonetheless.

Go'at handed Laila the lead saying, "*Amis-ennek*" (your camel, in Tamasheq). Laila reached out to take the lead and stroke his neck. She spoke his name with endearing enthusiasm and, before she knew it, his head came down. He started rubbing his cheek against the side of her head. He did it with such gusto it almost made her wonder if he wasn't equally glad to see her. Go'at laughed, as did she.

"I have never seen him so animated with a person," Go'at observed. "Or at least since Little Laila first rode him," he reminisced.

As Anarani continued to rub Laila's head, she giggled saying, "Well, he certainly knows how to welcome a person back!" Go'at pulled Anarani's lead toward him. Laila stepped to the side trying to smooth her hair into place again. She smelled of camel now. Blessed by Anarani, she thought. This was a good sign. Go'at directed Anarani, giving him a pat on his backside so he would join the other camels.

"Now," said Go'at, "we must replace your Western clothes. It is time to give you the *gandoras* and *sheshes* you ordered. They are all here as you requested."

"Thank you, Go'at. And you received the advance I sent you to cover these initial expenses?"

"Yes, it was more than enough and I was able to buy a new camel blanket for your saddle, which is much softer than the ones we nomads have grown used to. Nomads take pride in being very tough from our head to, well, you know," he chuckled. Laila loved how Go'at's eyes sparkled with mischief when he joked. Years ago, he and her father were like a comedy team, especially when relaxing after their formal duties were over. Although they were from such disparate backgrounds, they were in synch with each other's humor.

As they walked to where Go'at had his belongings, he introduced Laila to the other three nomads: Ouhetta, Ibrahim, and Epigee. Go'at was the cook, Ibrahim the tea maker, Epigee kept the equipment in order, and Ouhetta was the camel chief. But they all contributed to the necessary tasks in a caravan such as loading and unloading the camels, cooking, gathering firewood, making the fire, and finding the camels in the morning.

"*Ayouen*," they each greeted Laila in Tamasheq while extending their right hand for the Tuareg handshake—a quick brush of the palms and fingers. "*Ma tulam?*" (how are you), they asked. "*Imulen*," (well) Laila replied. Their *sheshes* were loosely wrapped, allowing their entire faces to be exposed. Not long ago this was unheard of, especially in the presence of a woman, much less a foreigner. But the ancient traditions of the Tuareg were unraveling. Here Laila stood with men whose blood ran as deep as the Saharan sand dunes. The depth of sand anchors the dunes just as the primal connection with this land anchors the Tuareg culture. But even external forces like the wind, or influences of the modern world, can affect their stability.

Ouhetta was the shortest, but had a powerful stance. His staccato steps spoke of swift determination. He knew the stark terrain like the back of his hand or the footprints of his camels. A caravan journey would always be sound with his guidance. Epigee stood tall and slim, and was nicknamed "Baggee" for the uncommonly disheveled way his *shesh* was wrapped. The volume of fabric encircling his head was baggy all around—top, sides, and across his face. One might think it was always on the verge of unraveling, except that when Laila watched him rewrapping it, the fabric ended up in as much disarray. Somehow it remained secure until the next wrapping. Ibrahim was the youngest. His handsome features were defined by an aquiline nose and eyes that were slightly lighter than the others, creating a piercing quality set in the darkness of his skin and hair. Ibrahim possessed a riveting smile that gleamed with straight, white teeth. His deep bass voice did not seem to match his slender build. Each man wore a moustache. Baggee's was the bushiest, while Ibrahim's was barely discernible. All were carrying the ancestry of the taller, lighter-skinned Arabic-featured Tuareg as opposed to that of the black African.

Once the introductions were finished, Go'at led Laila to his pack. He reached in for a large sack that contained the three separate *gandoras* and *sheshes* Laila had ordered. She had asked for the traditional colors of indigo, light blue, and white.

"There is one tent up where you can change," Go'at said as he pointed in its direction. Laila nodded grabbing her backpack and the sack. When she entered the tent, she sat for a moment to let settle the impact of traveling from one world to another and reconnecting with the past. The tent's interior was a cocoon of darkness and quiet. On the verge of replacing her urban clothes with desert attire, she felt at a transformational threshold: a final letting go of familiar cues on which she hung her identity. It was time to walk like a nomad–free, unbound, and as wide open as the sea of sand drifting in every direction.

Laila first pulled on the loose fitting elasticized pants over a pair of shorts. Then she slipped the matching white *gandora*, or long tunic, over her T-shirt. The neckline narrowed into a V-slit. It was edged with an ornately-embroidered white and beige bib with sequins sewn in teardrop leaf designs. Opening her backpack, she looked for the amulet that her father had given her only weeks before he died. He told her it was for protection. She wanted to wear it around her neck, and tucked it inside the front of the *gandora* to have close to her heart. Having donned the Tuareg attire, it was time to put her sandals back on. She walked out of the tent almost transformed carrying the *shesh*. She looked for Go'at.

"Go'at," she called out, "I need your help with the *shesh*." He came over and took the yards and yards of neatly folded white material Laila held out to him.

"My dad always wrapped the *shesh* when I wanted to wear it," Laila reminisced. "I loved when he did that for me."

As Go'at pulled up a portion to gently place over her head and frame her face, he looked in her eyes and replied, "I would be honored to teach you."

With no words, he started by bringing an edge of the material just below her chin and up so her lips could anchor it. Then he gently wrapped the rest of the fabric around her head and eventually across her face. When he reached the end on top of her head, he tucked it into the layers. One piece flowed in front that could be wrapped for extra protection when necessary. Go'at's touch was deft, tucking and arranging with careful precision.

Once Laila was fully enveloped, Go'at stepped back. They smiled, Go'at with his whole face, Laila with only her eyes. Draped in long, flowing, elegant clothing, she took a step forward moving with a regal gait. She then closed her eyes and lifted her arms, twirling slowly to feel how gracefully the material moved with her body and in the breeze. Go'at clapped his hands in delight.

"My dear Laila you look more like a Tuareg than a Tuareg looks like a Tuareg. It has not taken you long to again become one with our world." He paused. "You not only feel the desert, but the desert feels you." She bowed to his comments. He smiled back saying, "You are in the right place, and even though you may feel a pain that stabs like the thorns of the acacia tree, this could not be a more perfect time for you to be here."

Hearing his perceptive, loving words in her travel-weary and emotionally drained state, tears welled up. Go'at's fatherly care reminded her that circumstances never allowed her to show her own father how mature and strong she had become.

"I didn't want to cry," she blurted out. "You… you seem so much like my—" but she couldn't finish the sentence. "I'm sorry. I don't mean to be this emotional," Laila choked through her tears. Go'at came over, letting Laila rest her head on his shoulder as he comforted her.

"Don't you see that your tears are also perfect?" he asked. "Didn't you come here to feel what is buried deep inside? It will not be easy. So much of your history remains here and your healing is ready to happen. You have journeyed a long way for many reasons. But for now, come and relax with the setting sun, have some tea, and something to eat."

"Thank you, Go'at," she said lifting her head and taking a deep breath. "I'm very grateful for all you have done for me and my family. What a friend you are." She sniffled and realized that she had no tissues for her wet eyes and nose. Hesitantly, she wiped both with the end of her *shesh* looking over at Go'at with an embarrassed smile.

"Ahh," Go'at winked with approval, "you have also found another use for the *shesh*." His comment made her giggle. And with that, he extended his arm inviting Laila to lock her arm with his as they made their way to the fire. Ibrahim was brewing the tea. The pots with dinner sat on the glowing embers. This moment couldn't be any more inviting. Laila took her place around the fire and allowed the atmosphere to envelop her.

## LAILA'S JOURNAL ENTRY

The beautiful feature of the *shesh* is how it wraps the head so that only the eyes are revealed, allowing their unspoken language to be expressed with no other distractions. Eyes are richly expressive, enigmatic, and intense. They are the reflective reverie on the canvas of the face. There is an art to reading eyes framed as a still life, and eyes even in their stillness belie the restless soul that speaks from deep within.

Here I am with the Blue Men, soothsayers of the eyes. They not only read the emotions of the eyes, but also penetrate into the vulnerable core of their resident soul. When Go'at was teaching me how to wrap my *shesh*, I realized how my eyes and my heart have become wrapped in layers of protection over the years. Will I be able to unravel these layers guided by their wisdom? I already feel the *shesh*-wrapped vulnerability of my soul will be no match for their piercing perceptiveness.

## FALLING INTO THE VOID

As the morning sun slowly touched the edge of Laila's sleeping bag, she became aware of the clattering of pots. Go'at was reviving the fire and preparing breakfast. She spied the delicious bread left over from last night in a basket. Go'at baked the loaves according to the Tuareg tradition. He buried the dough in the sandy coals of the fire, with more embers placed on top. Laila felt home-baked bread held nothing over desert-baked bread.

With the bread and imminent tea enticing her, she sat up in her sleeping bag. But before going over, Laila knew it was time to take a first stab at wrapping her *shesh* the best she could from Go'at's example the prior day. She brought a shorter side over her head and held part of it in her mouth to anchor it. Next, she worked on wrapping 'round and 'round her head the dozen yards of the trailing fabric. Each advancing wrap was met with an equal amount of unwrap. It was all she could do to keep the long tail from also wrapping her torso. The fabric became so tangled that it looked like Baggee's *shesh*. Her frustration mounted when what she had wrapped on her head went so lopsided it partially fell off.

"Ugh!" Laila said emphatically, but under her breath. She looked over at the group and they seemed not to notice how out of control the fabric had gotten. She felt relieved. She then decided her next strategy would be to stand up so the fabric could have more room to flow. Laila began once again, this time trying to prevent herself from being entangled from the neck down. While she had a bit more success, in no way did the *shesh* feel secure. Again, she looked over at the group and this time she saw Go'at observing her with amusement. With her *shesh* in disarray over her head, she shrugged her shoulders and gave Go'at a disparaging look. He motioned for her to come over.

"I guess it takes a lot of practice," Laila said humbly.

"Of course! But do not forget that we learn as boys coming of age, and by that time we have already watched our fathers for many years. Not to mention how many generations it has been handed down, which may very well mean that we carry it in our blood. Be patient, dear Laila, be patient."

"Yes," she sighed, "I'll need to take that advice in more ways than for this. I remember when my father used to wrap my *shesh*. He told me to close my eyes while he wrapped it. Then when he was done, I could open them and he would have his *shesh* up so all I could see were his eyes. We then put our foreheads together so our eyes were right next to each other, and we would try to figure out what they were saying with the rest of our face covered. We would guess all kinds of things, but the last one that we always said was 'I love you'." She sighed again and smiled sadly at Go'at.

Go'at returned the smile and gently uncoiled what was left of the *shesh* atop her head, and with great patience slowly rewrapped it. Laila was in awe of just how much patience these nomads must have to live in so scarce an environment. She took a deep breath and closed her eyes. She tried to take in Go'at's gentle movements so she could absorb them from a place of sensing, rather than thinking. This reminded her how disconnected she had become from the deeper wisdom of her body. When Go'at was done, she opened her eyes.

"*Tenemert*, Go'at," (thank you, in Tamasheq).

"*Ayouen*," he responded. "And now time for some breakfast and tea."

Laila drank her tea while also drinking in the surrounding landscape. Where they camped was a hardened, flat, sandy surface with straggly bushes scattered here and there. Several feet beyond the campfire, the flat terrain rose up to a vertical landscape. The smattering of scrubby, green trees and bushes in the foreground gave way to a pile of rubbly stones and dark sand that abutted a high, marled rocky rise. Laila got up to survey the area closer. She remembered how she loved to sink her attention into an area like this when she was a child. There was so much to discover. Although the common notion of the Sahara Desert consists of endless sand and high dunes, in these Ahaggar Mountains the features of the desert change constantly. The variations provided tucked away coves or high rises, perfect for an anthropologist's daughter to climb. As she reminisced, she had to chuckle at the difference between the meaning of "high rise" in the desert and what it meant in the developed world.

✧✧✧

After breakfast and clean up, it was time to load and saddle the camels. The nomads worked swiftly and with great precision placing the supplies on the pack camels. This involved delicate balancing and equal distribution so no load was too heavy, not to mention securing the varying sized items in twine that they looped and tied. The saddles were also placed on the camels, just in front of their single hump. Of all the styles of camel saddles, only those from the Sahara are placed on the animals' shoulders using a wooden A-frame base. A saddle blanket went underneath to serve as a cushion for the camel. The backrest had a tall, shield-shape. In the front was a long tri-horned piece, much like Neptune's trident, serving as a handhold for stability. The flat, hard seat was made only slightly less uncomfortable for the rider when padded with a folded saddle blanket. The blankets were woven with a rough, woolen texture and had differing striped colors consisting of black, maroon, orange, yellow, white, and greens that ranged in hues from chartreuse to forest green to turquoise. In the middle was a line of colored, geometrical patterns.

As the nomads coaxed them to stand up, the camels' gravelly, fussing voices filled the air. Once assembled facing the direction of the day's journey, the caravan began its morning trek. Before mounting the camel, each person took the lead and walked for several minutes. When Laila was in the desert with her parents as a child, she was not expected to walk with the adults. So her father would place her on top of Anarani. She did not fear the height and delighted in being up so high in the sturdy Tuareg saddle.

Laila stepped out on this maiden voyage as an adult in the Sahara, the sun hanging low on the never-ending horizon. Immense sparseness saturated the desert world and way of life. Laila loved the surrounding simplicity as well as the nomads' unfettered lifestyle, although neither made for an easy existence.

As they began to walk, this morning's view held large, scrubby, green bushes and acacia trees that popped up from the sandy floor, set off by a low lying mountain range in the distance. None of the features rose up to any significant height. Flat sand strewn with stones and rocks gave way to vegetation that became widely dispersed tufts of brown grass and bushes. This view went on mile after mile. Even the mountains shrank into barely-perceptible undulations over the horizon.

Laila dreamed of being lost in the desert, journeying to a place she already knew. As she trekked into the Sahara, she was struck by feelings that were both exhilarating and foreboding. Her plans had delivered her to this point, but what waited beyond was as unpredictable as the wind. Where exactly was she going and what would she find? She was beginning to peel away layers, revealing what had brought her on this quest. Yes, some parts of this journey were about her father, but what seemed apparent was giving way to something deeper. She was following her soul's voice and heart's longing—the void into which she was choosing to fall.

Laila was familiar with being lost in the depths of her heart. Life as a single woman allowed her the freedom to go anywhere and to do anything. She was grateful for her free-spirited side that propelled her into the world with gusto. But there was a longing to feel her heart connected to another. Time and time again, she had endured the pain of losing what she thought was true love. Each breaking had left the darkened chambers of her heart exposed and gaping, much like the opened black walnut seedpods she would find on her walks in the woods back home. She would gaze at their chambers that resembled those of the heart, which would bring up what she longed for. Laila experienced these emotional wounds as a black hole, a turbulent, infinite haunting. Sometimes the denseness pulled her inward, tormenting every part of her being, and other times it fertilized her with a longing to wander the fields of pain that had been sown. This inner longing yearned for an outer landscape large enough to allow her to fall into the void of her heart; she needed to journey through a place that reflected the same vast starkness she felt within. This place could only be the largest desert in the world. She felt that every grain of sand and stony outcropping of this ancient land held insights to be discovered about the mysteries of life.

With a heavy sigh, Laila brought her wandering thoughts back to the moment. It was good to feel the sand beneath her feet. The loose scree made her feet and legs work harder when walking, strengthening the joints and muscles. She marveled at how robust the Tuareg were. Go'at seemed as agile as she remembered him twenty years ago. The caravan moved in silence. Only the shoosh, shoosh, shoosh of the camel pads on the sand and the whisper of a slight breeze were discernible.

With Anarani's lead rope draped over her shoulders, Laila became aware of how it felt to walk with such a large presence in tow. She felt comfortable knowing Anarani was just behind her. And with the angle of the sun they were also shadow-to-shadow, harmonized in a slow rhythmic pace. She felt as though he were already carrying her, even though she was not yet sitting in his saddle. He was a faithful companion, especially here where survival depended on these long-legged creatures carrying people to the next populated area. At this moment, Laila's heart was filled by the silent strength of Anarani, the nomads, and the desert. Yes, it was time to become lost on this journey of discovery.

## LAILA'S JOURNAL ENTRY

The Tuareg move in silence through the desert. They are tuned in to the subtlest gestures from each other as well as the far-flung landmarks in their environment. Such silence is unheard of back home where white noise hovers in the air, emanating from every corner and nook. No escapes, even to the forests or the ocean, are as quiet as this desert, save when the wind blows. Where silence permeates life, one preserves it, much like those steeped in noise readily plug in to modern distractions.

Heat, wind, and bone-chilling cold do not promote small talk, but they do heighten awareness of how close to an edge one lives. A nod of the head, a glance of the eye, or a movement of the hand conveys essential messages. Already my time here is bringing up the cacophony of my inner voices, including those speaking of my father's death. People back home couldn't comprehend my venturing back to a place where I must confront these memories once again.

## A TIME OF REBELLION

When Laila was ready to ride Anarani, Ouhetta came over to couch him so she could climb into his saddle. She removed her sandals and strapped them together. Ouhetta took them from her so he could loop them into the series of ropes that held the saddle. He then cupped his hands together, giving her a foothold to swing her leg over the tall saddle. This was the inexperienced style of mounting. The Tuareg are very adept at the acrobatics of mounting while their camels are standing or even when walking. But Laila loved the awkward, exaggerated back and forth, carnival ride sensation of Anarani as he stood up.

"*Tenemert*," she said.

"*Ayouen*," he responded with a nod.

"Ouhetta," Laila said as the caravan started to move again. He strode alongside Anarani.

"Yes, Laila."

"How old is Anarani?"

"Well that is a question I must think on." Ouhetta's eyes squinted in thought for a second then said, "He is the years of my son who was born around the same time."

"Do you know how many years that is?"

"Oh, we do not follow our age as you do from the West. That is not our tradition."

"But your son is a young man, right?"

"He is a man, yes. He went to the city to study. He did not want to be a camel herder like his father."

"Did you want him to follow in your footsteps?"

"I want him to do what works in this world now. When I grew up, I did as my father and his father before him, and so on. Now, so many outside influences weigh upon us, and the rebellions…" his voice trailed off. "There are many changes to our way of life, so he must choose from what it is like now, not what I once lived. And as a camel trainer, I know that the only way you have success training a camel is to work with its nature. If you try to force the hand, that is when camels rebel and spit, and none of my camels do that."

"It sounds very complicated and you are very wise," Laila said. She thought of the circumstances that were forced on her life from the rebellion. In that moment, Laila felt Ouhetta as a kindred soul.

The caravan glided fluidly over the sand, their pace as lazy as the day was hot. In the distance, the wide valley of sand they traversed was demarcated on either side by slight ridges of hills topped by jagged crests. In this expansive landscape, Laila felt how small her presence was. This was both humbling and freeing. The world was made to allow the wildness of one's soul to co-mingle with the wildness of nature. Never an easy journey. But there were moments, like the caravan's pace, that allowed for quiet connection and contemplation.

✦✧✦

As the ride wound down for the day, the caravan arrived at an area with very little vegetation. There was no foliage for the camels to forage. So once the gear and saddles were removed, the men couched the camels and laid out grains for the camels' meal. It looked as if they were being served in a restaurant.

Laila observed the orchestrated movements of the nomads. Each man meticulously performed his task in harmony with the others, gliding with lightning quickness to set up for the evening's camp. She spied Baggee gathering all the twine from the camel saddles and packs. He draped each one around his neck until he had a multitude of long strands almost dragging on the ground. Their yellow color contrasted with the blue of his *gandora* and enhanced his already disheveled appearance. Then he neatly wound each strand with great care to ensure they did not get entangled. Ouhetta broke apart branches that had been tied together and carried along, specifically for such a place as this with nothing to burn in sight. Go'at's focus was on creating a kitchen area, which was a series of mats laid out surrounded by boxes of utensils, cookware, and food. And, as customary, there was the tea. Ibrahim set out all of his tea making materials that were carried in plastic shopping baskets, and started a small fire for brewing.

Laila decided to walk over to Anarani. His long neck extended straight out from his body allowing his mouth to slurp the pile, and when it was full, he raised his head to chew. Laila petted his neck.

He stopped chewing in response, as if he was savoring her touch. She wasn't sure, but it almost seemed as if he had something to say to her during his pauses. His eyes gazed out expressive, soft, and pensive. Then again, camels' eyes have an inherently enigmatic quality so it was easy to anthropomorphize.

"It's good to see you again, Anarani," she said as much to release her internal gratitude as to convey it to him. She was amazed at the overwhelming sense of coming home she felt in a land she had not lived in for so many years. The feeling wasn't just about the childhood memories the Sahara evoked, but about how deeply it filled her awareness in the present moment. Settling in next to Anarani's shoulders, she pulled her knees up, wrapped her arms around them, and took in the waning day. As far as she could see the horizon was unobstructed. Earth and sky never lost touch with each other. Whether the terrain was composed of sand, rocks, or mountains, every inch of the curves and edges below candidly consorted with the expansive space above. An uncluttered environment allowed one to just be. The austerity permeated the senses. It was a bit like osmosis—the density of inner thoughts and worries diluted by the outer vastness and beauty. Maybe, Laila thought, I am opening my heart and mind to find comfort not just in the external surroundings, but also within my own skin.

With the sun's last rays, Laila took a deep breath, got up, gave Anarani a final rub on top of his head, and made her way to join the group at the fire, where dinner was cooking and tea was brewing.

✧✦✧

Eating in the Tuareg tradition took on a closeness not found in the Western world. The contents of dinner were served in medium-sized enamel bowls. This evening, one held a salad of lettuce, carrots, beets, and tomatoes tossed with oil and vinegar. The other bowl held chopped spaghetti with sauce. However, the food was not portioned out into individual bowls. First, the salad bowl was placed in the middle of the four men and Laila. Each person had a fork. Usually the Tuareg used their fingers to eat, but they were honoring Laila's early immersion back into their culture. Everyone ate within one area of the bowl. They joked, saying each person had to eat from their own "garden." Putting the handle of a fork into the sand indicated that a person was finished eating. If all the forks ended up in the sand, and someone wanted to finish what was left, then that person could eat from the other "gardens." Once everyone finished the salad, they sat around the pasta eating from their garden in that bowl.

Laila was surprised at how hungry she was. The men ate very slowly, and they didn't completely finish their garden. When they stuck the handles of their forks in the sand, Laila was still eating her portion. Her eyes spied what was left. Go'at noticed and began to chuckle. When she looked up at him, he circled his finger around the bowl then pointed to her. She felt a bit embarrassed at her hunger, but she took his lead and ate the rest.

"Laila," Go'at wanted to reassure her, "it is always best to finish food and not have leftovers. While we can keep fresh food from going bad, it becomes harder with prepared food. What we do not eat, we feed to the camels. So there will never be any waste." She nodded weighing out how she felt about eating what might have gone to the camels. Maybe she would choose to be less hungry tomorrow.

Once dinner was over, Go'at pulled out his guitar (which was always within reach) to lead the men in a song that sounded ancient and haunting, although like modern blues. This was a style Laila didn't remember hearing when she was a child.

"Go'at?"

"Yes, Laila."

"I don't remember hearing any music like that when I was here with my parents. Where does this style come from?" Go'at told her of the time of the Tuareg rebellion when she and her mother left the Sahara.

"War does not bring much in the way of benefits, but the clash of viewpoints and beliefs can also introduce new ideas that may enhance the culture of a people," he began. "With settlements being forced on the traditional nomadic lifestyle, many young people became completely lost and without direction. From these external pressures, especially the government restrictions on our need to seek pastures for our herds amid endless droughts, a whole generation of youth left their families to find a means of survival. Borders enforced by the government meant they had to 'go abroad.' That is a foreign concept to we who see land as shared, open, and for all to wander. We are a people who do not understand asking permission to move.

"Thus, the Tuareg, who once lived in a world without walls, became ethnic minorities dwelling within the boundaries of five different countries: Libya, Algeria, Niger, Mali, and Burkina Faso. This led to Tuareg cultural resistance. During the Tuareg rebellion, young men who were in military training camps outside of their designated 'country' came into contact with other lifestyles and expressions. This is where the electric guitar was introduced. They learned this instrument, brought it back, and integrated it into the culture. We call this contemporary music '*Ishumaren*' and it is linked to the movements of exile and resistance. It encouraged and roused young Tuareg, called *Ishumar*, to come together and fight in order to revive the dignity of the Tuareg people.

"The *Ishumar* may move around, but not in the traditional nomadic style. They move here and there, sometimes to find opportunities to work. Other times they have no purpose. The nomadic life is one with purpose—for salt trade, for livestock, to find water. Their life is lived mostly in the moment, disorganized, and disengaged from traditions. But the one thing that unites their sense of being is the style of music that was influenced by the rebellion."

Laila mulled over the fragile resilience of this tale and what it meant in her own life. "We really lost touch with the details of the rebellion after we left. Once we got back home, my mother and I focused on readjusting to our lives without my father. We hardly talked about our Saharan experiences and it was hard for us to hear reports about the area, especially for my mother."

"That is understandable," Go'at empathized.

"I hope," Laila contemplated, "that the symbolism and depth of the music was only part of the positive impact from the rebellion."

Go'at said the good news was how the rebellion ended with peace accords in 1995 and 1996. "However," he continued, "while we hoped to gain equal rights that called for fair distribution of wealth and resources, provisions for education, access to jobs, and representation in government bodies, these promises ended up like the proverbial trans-Saharan highway. There are many who still live as refugees because no means of subsistence or any other infrastructure are in place for them to come home to. And more recently, with growing frustration at these deteriorating conditions, there have been uprisings in Niger. Without sustainable policies, it's like making braids on top of lice, as an old Tuareg saying goes."

He paused when Ouhetta asked for help to gather up the grain bags, then continued speaking to Laila as he got up. "But the dignity of our culture runs deep. Our strong sense of belonging is much more ancient and meaningful than the outside influences that dictate the conditions around us. This is our strength, and we must feed our children the passion of the desert so it becomes part of their soul even as they become more exposed to modern influences." With that, Go'at turned to walk with Ouhetta.

## LAILA'S JOURNAL ENTRY

It is time to learn more about the rebellion that altered the course of my life. I have always been afraid of the pain it might bring up about Dad's death, but I can't avoid that dark place anymore. Like the definitive horizon around me, I want to clarify the reasons I am compelled to return to this setting at this point in time. It might be empowering to seek clarity. But it will not be easy to integrate the knowledge I may find, for it will remove the shadows of confusion in which I have hidden.

## SWEET LIKE DEATH

The men chatted and laughed while cleaning up after dinner. Laila helped Go'at wash dishes in the "kitchen." Ibrahim had already poured two rounds of the tea. Laila was served her tea while she was dunking the bowls and forks and handing them to Go'at for drying. He placed the last of the dried utensils in their boxes.

"Thank you, Laila. Now, let's enjoy the rest of this beautiful evening."

Go'at picked up his guitar again, sat down at the fire and began strumming. He experimented with a few bars until he launched into a repetitive melody. The men meditatively gazed at the fire. A slight breeze stirred. In harmony with the guitar, the men hummed "uh-oh, uh-oh." Their voices droned in a breathy, guttural, low then high tone on each of the syllables. The breeze shifted toward the fire, like a small whirlwind. The embers swirled upward into tiny, glowing, dancing fireflies, arising in a flash and suddenly gone.

As the men's hushed chanting softly flowed, Ibrahim walked

around the circle to pour the third round of tea. Laila was drawn into the spell of the tea ceremony, but she was not feeling her awareness loosening beyond the glow of the fire, the voices of the nomads, and the surrounding desert darkness. Her mind was too engaged. She was hoping their singing would sink into her heart to help her feel, rather than think, the answers she was seeking. She took a deep breath and closed her eyes to focus on their voices. As she relaxed, her thoughts began to ebb, bringing a sense of space between one and the next.

When Laila opened her eyes again, Ibrahim stood before her with his teapot. He had not yet poured the tea in her glass. She looked up. His eyes gazed into hers. With a smile on his lips, he poured the tea and nodded his head. The men stopped singing in response.

"Ibrahim," Go'at said, "tell Laila the story of making the tea."

Ibrahim walked back to his place in the circle and poured his own cupful, arching the spout high to create the foam in his glass. Everyone drank the final round in silence and looked toward Ibrahim to tell his story.

"When I brew the tea, I use the same leaves for all three rounds. In the first round, it is the nature of the tea to be bitter. As I continue to brew, bitterness gives way to a strong, but mellow flavor. And as I brew the tea the third and final time, the leaves and flavor naturally weaken. If I were to serve the tea itself, I doubt that it would be pleasing, so I add another ingredient to enhance and transform its flavor: sugar for sweetness.

"When we brew our lives, we do so with the same body and mind, heart and soul. We learn early on that life has a bitter nature. As we grow and take on the world, life tests our strength physically and emotionally and with time we find that our bodies naturally weaken. If this were all that life was about, what pleasures would it hold? Oh, to brew our lives in the same way that we brew tea. It takes conscious effort to add sweetness. With a sweetened outlook, the misfortunes that inevitably come to us are more likely to be transformed, just as I transform the bitterness and strength and weakness of the tea with sugar. By using a conscious mind and the strength of love in our hearts and souls, we have the chance to let go of the wounds we received. Choosing such a path is not easy but it is one that can enhance life. Those who do not choose such a path may find the final round, death, is not so sweet. To experience the sweetness of death takes a lifetime of opening our hearts." Ibrahim closed his eyes and the men resumed their chanting.

Laila felt the truth of his words penetrate her heart, and when his eyes opened they locked with hers. She could not look away. His eyes beckoned her toward him and in a flash she was transported back to a world she knew as a child.

❁☼❁

Laila finds herself remotely viewing a nomadic camp in Algeria near the Niger border. In this scene are her father, mother, and herself as a child. They are walking and talking with the people. She understands enough to know they are expressing words of sadness at leaving the country due to something called the "Tuareg revolution." Suddenly, gunshots ring out. People are screaming and scattering. Caught in the crossfire, her father instinctively grabs her and, with her mother, they run into a tent for protection. However, fearing the fighting might get closer, her dad tells them he is going to find a more secure hiding place. He keeps his body low while running between tents to stay out of view of the shooters and reaches a craggy outcropping of stones. He finds a safer haven, but as he makes his way back to his family, a stray bullet finds him. It is hard for Laila to view this scene for she knows it is lethal and that it would have been best to stay put because the skirmish subsides within minutes.

Go'at, Jack's key informant and right-hand man, finds Katherine and Laila huddling inside the tent sick with worry. They tell Go'at that he left them to look for a place to hide. Go'at leads them to another tent where the women are gathering and then heads in the direction that Katherine last saw her husband running.

It doesn't take Go'at long to find Jack lying on the ground, blood covering his chest. Their eyes lock. Laila remembers the very close bond they had, working so many years with each other. She observes the depth of their bond in these final moments of her father's life and, as much as she wants to look away, her eyes are riveted on the scene. With no exchange of words, Go'at knows he must do all he can to keep his good friend's family safe and help them get back home. With a heavy heart, he carries Jack's limp, bleeding body into the camp and places him in a tent, then goes to tell his family.

When Go'at returns to their tent, Katherine's arm is around

Laila holding her tight to her side. The air is thick with the tense, nervous energy of uncertainty about who may have succumbed to the shooting. Go'at approaches Katherine and shares with her what he knows. Katherine stares straight ahead in disbelief then pulls Laila even closer and whispers in her ear letting her know that she must stay put. Go'at brings one of the young girls over to look after Laila then takes Katherine to the tent where her father lies. Laila struggles watching these events unfold. Not being in her body, she has no ability to disengage from what she is viewing.

The next thing she sees is her mother rushing to her father's body, disbelief expanding into overwhelming grief, knowing that not only his blood, but also his life, have seeped out through that one small hole in his chest. Numb and distraught with shock, Katherine embraces Jack's body. Laila knows that from this point forward their life together will move at warp speed in order to make their way home, a broken unit. Katherine looks up at Go'at, tears streaming down her face, and she seems to find the slightest comfort in his expressive eyes. She takes her husband's hand in hers, kisses it, then kisses his lips. She wants to cry harder, but parental duty and instinct take over. She must carry the strength of two people now. As she gets up to go to Laila, she lays a hand on Go'at's shoulder. He places his hand over hers and gently squeezes it, letting her know he will keep vigil until she returns.

Laila then sees herself playing a traditional board game using stones and date pits with the young woman who is caring for her. When her mother reappears, Laila looks up and sees her mother's expression. It frightens her. Katherine tells Laila that her father went the way of the old man who died in the tribe not too long ago. He is no longer as he used to be. Laila doesn't know what to think, but her mother says that she will take her to see her father as he is now. Katherine holds out her hand, attempting to produce a reassuring smile. Laila takes her hand and the two walk apprehensively together. At the tent's opening, Katherine tells Laila to stand and wait for just a moment. She enters, and finds that Go'at was able to remove the bloody shirt and had covered Jack's body with camel blankets. Then she goes to the entrance to get Laila.

Ten-year-old Laila thinks that her father is sleeping and gently taps his cheeks with her fingers. She wants to wake him so that he knows she is there, but her mother tearfully explains that he is unable to wake up. Laila looks up at her mother and Katherine tells her that her father has died and is no longer in his body. Laila puts the palms of her hands on both sides of her father's face and squeezes his cheeks. She wants to make him breathe. She can't understand. Only moments ago he was with them. Katherine explains that a bullet took his life away. Crying, she kneels in front of Laila and hugs her. Laila leans over her mother's shoulder. There are no tears of sadness when you are viewing the one you love and have yet to comprehend that you will never hear the joy of his voice or feel the warmth of his touch again.

---

Then, suddenly, the intense clarity of this vision from Laila's past evaporated. Not only had she recounted hazy memories, but the gaps in knowledge were filling in like mortar. As Laila's eyes refocused on her current surroundings, she found herself leaning against Go'at. She turned to him, tears in her eyes.

"Have I been gone long?" she asked him.

"Not long. I was here with you the entire time," he said as he gave her shoulders a reassuring squeeze with his arm.

Laila tried to gather her wits, but she still felt steeped in the timeframe of the vision. The tears flowed down her cheeks. Staring into the fire, her mind produced memories of the next several days after the shooting. They were a blur to both her mother and her, but for different reasons. Katherine was immersed in a swirl of activity, having to report this crisis to the authorities while making the arrangements to pack up for home. Laila observed the activity going on all around her, not knowing what to do. Much of her time was spent with the young girl who was with her when her father was shot. Go'at had arranged to have her watch over Laila so Katherine could focus on the logistics of leaving.

Before they left this part of the world, her mother had to honor her husband's wish. Jack wanted to be cremated and brought back to the Sahara so his ashes could mix with the limitless grains of sand, becoming one with the shifting dunes, and carried far and wide by the desert winds. Laila realized that he didn't have to come back. He had arrived not ever having to leave. As much anguish as this caused her and her mother, it propelled Laila on a life's journey she might not have walked had events not unfolded as they had. She had not previously thought of this tragedy as a gift but, as Ibrahim so wisely pointed out, even death can be sweetened if we so choose.

## A STRANGE CONVERSATION

Sitting close to the fire writing in her journal, Laila was grateful for the morning's slow start since it gave her time to turn over the previous day's experiences in her mind. Besides, she was not so fond of the morning chill and it gave her a chance to soak up the warmth of the flames. Their breakfast of bread, dates, and tea had already been passed around. The men were still eating and lingering in conversations. Laila was sitting in singular quietude, a more familiar state of being to her.

As she stared off, she saw a lone camel hobbling close to where the packs were scattered. From this distance, she could see the scars on his face and knew it was Anarani. He was closer than any camel usually comes at this time of the morning, as they remain farther out until the men herd them back. He continued to approach then stopped, looking her direction intently. Laila felt compelled to walk over to him.

"Good morning, my regal boy," she said as she gently rubbed his cheek. She opened her hand with a few dates she had taken from the basket. His soft, furry lips sucked them up. Laila smiled at the exaggerated back and forth movements of the camel jaw.

"You're such a good boy. Yes, you are." She stroked his long neck, butting and rubbing her head against him as well. He liked this and lowered his chin to rub on her *sheshed* head. It made the precarious wrapping start to unwind, given Laila was still at the beginner's stage. After several minutes, she gave him one last head butt and a hug around the neck. Then she turned to go back to the fire.

She had not gotten but a few steps when she heard a voice from behind her say, "Sing the song." It didn't sound quite human. She turned slowly and sure enough, there stood Anarani, only Anarani. His jaws were no longer moving, but his eyes seemed to search her face. Laila put her hands on her hips and cocked her head to one side. Then she walked toward him.

"Anarani?"

"Laila?" he responded in a hoarse, gravelly tone.

She stopped short in her approach. Puzzlement increased to

incredulity.

"Anarani?"

"Laila?" If she had any doubt that his mouth formed her name the first time, her direct view of him this time put that doubt to rest.

"Anarani…"

"Are we sure of each other's name?" he asked cutting her off. Laila looked around to see if any of the men were heading their direction. Two of them were busy gathering the packs while the other two had gone off to gather the camels.

"You understand me and can talk?" she asked.

"Well, since your family left here there have been people who speak English traveling with this caravan, so I have listened and practiced, yes."

"But that aside, you're a camel and camels are not usually able to speak at all except, I guess, maybe Camel," she suggested.

"I've been telling myself that ever since I was as high as my mother's knee." One eyelid lowered as the other rose. Laila had never seen such an expression on a camel.

"Does anyone here know about this?" Laila pointed in the direction of the campsite.

"No. If you are seen here, no good comes of it."

"But you are letting me see you."

Lowering his head so their eyes met, Anarani responded, "I believe the word is 'trust'?" He raised his head back up, shook it, paused, and started chewing his cud. Laila continued to stand there dumfounded. But as she gazed at this whimsical, doey-eyed, dragon beast, it shifted to bemusement. Somehow, in the grand scheme of this journey and this place, hearing a camel talk did not seem as strange as it would have anywhere else.

"Laila!" she heard Go'at call her name. "Come. Bring Anarani. We must prepare to leave!" She waved in response and turned back to Anarani.

"I guess we need to join the group."

"Seems so," he agreed.

They gazed at each other. Laila stepped toward Anarani, reaching out her hand. Anarani snuffled her palm with his snout then gave her a gentle nudge on her *shesh*. "Well Anarani, my dear talking camel, I can't believe I am saying this to you, but, 'shall we'?" she asked holding her arm out in an inviting gesture. Anarani moved forward, but his front ankles were still hobbled.

"Wait, let me take that off," Laila said. She bent down to unwrap the binding. As she pulled it off, she remembered what started this strange exchange.

"You said, 'sing the song'. What did you mean?" She came around to the front of him so she could loop the rope around his neck.

"Remember long ago when your father lifted you onto me to ride and you sang my name over and over? Then you sang it in my ear while rubbing my cheeks?"

The memory came flooding back into Laila's mind. She hadn't thought of that tune since she was a child. A sudden rush of warmth mixed with sadness arose at the thought, for it also brought up memories of her father.

"Do you remember that song?" Anarani asked. Laila felt his stare.

"How could I forget?" she answered, her eyes teary. "Of course I'll sing my song! I'll sing it once I am on your back feeling the rhythm of your walk."

Laila and Anarani walked slowly toward Go'at, her hand on his neck to look like she was guiding him. Ibrahim approached to attach the rope to Anarani's nose ring and led him to the area where all the camel saddles were laid out. Gone was the calm of the morning. Breaking camp was the most energetic part of the day. The men moved about speaking or signaling information to each other. The camels, especially those being loaded with the supply packs, groaned in response. Laila could only describe their voices as sounding like Chewbacca from Star Wars, so the idea that she just had a conversation with such a beast took on an even greater absurdity. Her mind was still in disbelief at the exchange.

Laila joined Go'at, who was squatting down putting out the fire with sand. He looked up at her and commented, "Your face has the look of one who has experienced a *djinn*. Is something wrong?"

Laila remembered the *djinn* are spirits, or genies, of the desert. Some are bad and hurt people, others good and helpful. In the desert legends they don't live in bottles that must be rubbed for their release. They can lurk anywhere or possess anyone.

"And how is it I look?" she asked.

"Confused, like the *djinn* told or showed you something that held great contradiction," Go'at replied.

"I think there's just a lot going on inside of me about my father and returning to the place where I last saw him," she said. She hoped her response, which sidestepped the more immediate truth, sounded convincing.

"Yes, yes, this can make many feelings well up. But when we are called to venture closer to the bitterness of our lives, emotions can be much like the wells of the desert. It may take some time to find them and, when you do, what lies beneath runs deep. You must be willing to bring what courses below to the surface or you will live with a thirst that never goes away."

"But what if you drink and drink and the thirst still doesn't go away? I have felt a longing in my heart not only to come back here, but also to find some way to make sense of my life. Being here helps me live right now, in the moment. That is how I want to live, but our modern world is so complicated and full of damage and distractions."

"Here is not so free of complications either," Go'at said. "We may still look like we are living life as it has been for generations. But the truth is that the only way we are able to have an existence like this is through tourists. Sometimes they come and sometimes they do not."

Laila squatted down to look squarely at him. "Go'at, I have never seen you have a bad day," she recalled. "Yet I know you must have gone through hard times especially through the revolution. I admire how you take it all in and still have a sense of humor. I saw how you did that when you worked for my father."

"We are a people who live in the wake of the dunes where nothing is given save the wind, the sand, and the sun. We must find humor. I think you describe it as black humor. There is a saying about the life of a Tuareg. Life has three stages: one day you are happy, the next day you are sad, and the third day you are dead. Living is living come what may."

Laila rested her head on her hand. "You are right," she contemplated. "It's not just living for the moments when they are filled with blessings. It's also having patience to live every second of uncertainty without trying to shift it to certainty. It's being able to embrace the unknown and the longing while not being drowned by them."

"Then you are surely in the right place to embrace the

unknown and the longing because," Go'at put his arms out and looked up at the sky, "the chances of drowning in the middle of this desert steeped in many years of droughts is very, very small, don't you think?" The material of his *shesh* was below rather than across his face, so Laila could see his sardonic smile along with the usual twinkle in his eyes.

Laila gave an exaggerated ha-ha. "Here I guess I could 'cry me a river' as an old song says and my tears would probably evaporate before they even touched the ground," she said, following his line of jest.

Go'at buried the last of the burnt remains in the sand, sat back on his heels, and clapped his hands together to get the sand off. She then saw his eyes shift to a point beyond her saying, "It looks like we are ready to begin our day's journey."

Laila turned around to see the men prodding the saddled and loaded camels up from their resting positions. She saw Anarani standing there, chewing his cud, his saddle strapped in front of his hump. He looked like an unremarkable camel with no hint of awareness beyond that of the other camels. Go'at and Laila got up and they started walking.

"My dear Go'at, I don't know how I could do this without you," her voice conveyed a cheery tone on the verge of tears.

"You would be doing this no matter what," Go'at wisely affirmed. "I am only serving as a witness and a guide."

Once they reached the assemblage of men and camels, Ouhetta gave Anarani's lead rope to Laila. She stood close against his chest and neck awaiting the signal to move. Laila placed a hand on Anarani's neck. Just moments ago she had a verbal exchange with him… hadn't she? As they started to walk, Anarani lumbered along, his eyes roving with no particular focus in stark contrast to how expressive they had been earlier when he spoke.

The caravan drifted into an easy pace. At least two of the nomads walked along with the pack camels. It was hard for Laila to fathom that they were walking in any particular direction given the horizon was directionless every way she looked. There was barely a landmark to catch her eyes, but the Tuareg's knowledge is based on generations of partnership with sand, dunes, rocks, and expansive sky. Nothing escapes their keen observations.

The configuration of the caravan was shaped by the landscape, morphing to the features like an amoeba. The wide expanse allowed drifting of the camels into a wider, looser formation. Then as they came to areas scattered with numerous large rocks piled in close proximity, the camels channeled into a single file.

When it was time to mount for riding, Laila was feeling more excited than usual to be in the saddle having received the request from Anarani. Once she settled in the saddle and the caravan started moving, Laila allowed herself to sink into the rhythm of Anarani's long-legged walk. As an adult, her bare feet could rest on his U-shaped neck. She imagined Anarani's front legs as extensions of her hips, striding like a model down the runway. She straightened her back and felt her body gently swaying to his legs as each reached out to one side, then to the other. There was a soothing quality to the movement. If only the saddles were not so hard on the backside, she thought, you could almost feel like you were being rocked in a cradle.

In the calmness of her mind, the song Anarani had requested gradually bubbled up from her memories and she started to hum it softly. She hummed it through a few times. The only lyrics she had come up with as a child was singing his name over and over. She began singing and noticed that he turned his head around shaking it. Was this an acknowledgement of her singing? There could be no full acknowledgement in the presence of others. His wish was not to be seen, for there was no telling what his fate would be if people caught wind of a talking camel.

✧✧✧

As the day's journey came to an end, the men began unloading the camels and setting up the fire for tea, food, and warmth. Anarani knelt down to let Laila slide off. She scratched his ear and gave him a wink. He winked back as Baggee loosened and pulled off his saddle. Laila got close to Anarani's ear and whispered in it, "Were you happy I sang the song?" He nodded his head in response. She petted the side of his face.

It was time to let the camels loose to forage for vegetation. Anarani stood up and Laila took off the cord that hung around his neck so she could hobble his front ankles. She hated doing this knowing he had the wherewithal to return in the morning. Maybe she could try to convince the group to let him be? But for now, she did what was expected.

## ANARANI

Laila was anxious to talk more with Anarani, but how with the requirement of not being heard? Luck would have it that they came to rest in an area that had many stone outcroppings and large boulders lying about. She thought maybe she could tell the group that she was going off to write in her journal until dinner. She fished it out once her pack was unloaded and let Go'at know in which direction she was headed. She pursued Anarani before he got too far away.

The camels had rounded a high stone mound with a plateau top. There were a number of scrubby bushes and acacia trees in this setting; Anarani's very long neck was stretching up to munch one of the thorny branches. Laila approached him.

"Anarani," she half whispered. He looked her way in mid-chew. His eyebrows took on a worried furl. He couldn't quite talk with his mouth full, nor did he trust talking so close to the men. Backing up from the tree with his eyes on Laila, he nodded his head to one side hoping she would understand to follow him. Then he turned to walk. Laila kept a few paces back while looking behind to make sure no one had kept watch of her.

They walked where large boulders were piled up and resting against a high wall of stone. Anarani rounded the cluster and sat down on the flat sand. Laila came over and sat on one of the boulders next to him. Being concealed, Laila spoke up.

"Anarani, I can't help but wonder how you can talk. Have you always been able to? Can you tell me your story?"

He drew in a deep camel breath, shook his head back and forth, and began. "Not always. I was like any camel that would someday carry packs or people. Ouhetta favored me because I was good-natured. I followed his commands when I was young, so he trained me as a camel to carry people. Camels who get excited or fight, they are made to carry the packs. If you do not follow the commands of your owner, you will never have the honor to carry him on your back.

"Do you see the young camels tied together that walk with us?" Laila nodded. "They are camels in training learning the ways of the caravan. I was once tied like that as a young camel on a caravan learning the rhythm and words of the nomads many sunrises ago. But there was one caravan that changed my life forever." Anarani's eyes shifted to a far off gaze.

"We had walked three days and nights and on the fourth day, deep into the desert, a sandstorm came. It was the worst I have seen in all of my days, with a wall of sand many, many caravans long and as high as the sun. It moved faster than a camel in a race. How strong it was. And yet, there was only one thing to do—sit and wait for it to pass. It was very hard for Ouhetta and the other men to couch the camels. Everyone was nervous, especially we camels. We all wanted to run.

"Ouhetta came to the three of us, but the approaching storm stirred the sand up under our feet and we were leaping around. He could not keep hold of our leads, the knots became loose, and we broke free. The wall was so close and my fear blinded me. I ran straight into it."

"What happened then?"

"If you have a hard time believing that I talk, then you will not believe what happened next," he said as he cocked his head toward Laila.

"What, what?"

"Inside that wall, there was no wind and sand. I was in a space filled with calm. The grains of sand and air were still. I shook my head and blew the sand out of my nose. Then a woman dressed in an indigo veil and flowing robes appeared. She had white hair and eyes that sparkled. They made me trust her. She floated toward me. Her robes gave off light. In her hand were thin strands of green grass. The smell was so sweet that it made my mouth water. It was like no scent I had ever smelled before.

"She held out her hand and I did not hesitate to eat. The grass was not dry, but moist and tender! She smiled sweetly rubbing my ear. I ate and ate. The grass never ended. Then the woman pulled her hand away and I suddenly found myself staring at a field filled with tall green grass. This was a place I had never seen before. Green grass growing as far as my eyes could see. The woman was no longer with me, but I now could eat all the grass I wanted. I ate and ate until I was full. It made me very, very tired so I sat down and stretched my neck out to rest on the cool earth dreaming of this magical place and the woman who fed me.

"The next thing I heard was the voices of the men. I raised my head full of sand and shook it. I saw the vast desert, not the green grass. The men had me stand and took me back with the rest of the caravan now that the sandstorm had passed.

"The woman was a *djinn* and from that day, I became a different camel. I began to hear the language of the people, to understand it. My voice sounded different, too. I tried to hide it because I was afraid the people and the other camels would think I was odd. I knew that it was best to fit in." He paused and began chewing his cud.

Laila had no words. Not only was this an unbelievable story, it was even more so the way in which she was hearing it. All she could do was reach her hand out to stroke Anarani's neck. They lingered like this for several minutes, Anarani chewing his cud and Laila stroking his neck, both enjoying the waning day and their time together, made all the more rich by this fantastic sharing. As they continued to sit in silence, Laila mulled over what she had heard. She knew the desert could play tricks on the eyes with mirages, but this, this was phantasmagorical! And right now it was her reality.

"Anarani."

"Yes, Laila."

"Tell me more about your life and being able to talk."

"After the *djinn* and tasting the magical grass in the sandstorm, I tried to find ways to practice my new gift. Working on the caravans I had time away from ears that might hear me using my voice. At the end of the day, I walked farther out than the other camels to speak the words I heard spoken between the men, your father, and from my master Ouhetta.

"At first I practiced with only my name, 'Ahh-nahh-rahh-neeee.'" He brought his head near Laila's ear on the "neeee" and she giggled. "It took many nights to finally not sound so much like a camel. Then when my voice became less well—camel, I was excited to learn new words. Every morning I walked to the camp before the men herded the other camels back. The men made much noise and tried to keep me away. They thought I was looking for food, but I stood wherever I heard a conversation and they finally got used to me. Even in the village I made my way close to the tent where the children sat to learn lessons from the elders. Men led me away to be with the other camels, but once they turned their backs, I outsmarted them. They finally gave up. What harm was one camel?"

"You know English and Tamasheq so well. What a great accomplishment. You are very smart." Laila observed.

"*Parlez vous francaise?*" Laila saw a smirk on his wide camel lips.

"*Oui.* So you know French also?"

"I knew there were different sounds the men used and there was another by your mother and father. But what else does a camel have to do with the same desert passing by? I always listened to what people said in the caravan and in the villages. It was not that hard. What people need to say is not that different, even if the sounds are different, don't you agree?" He looked squarely at Laila.

"Good observation, my dear, intelligent dromedary," she smiled back.

"What is that word you called me?"

"Well, you are a very smart camel, so..."

"No, no, not intelligent, the other one. Dromo..."

"Oh, you are a camel with one hump on your back, so you are a dromedary camel. Then there are camels with two humps and they are called Bactrian camels."

"Humpf! Two humps! That is a joke?!" his eyes widened. Laila laughed.

"No, it's true, but they live much farther east from here." She paused then asked, "Anarani, can you tell me why you have those scars on your cheeks?"

Anarani was lost in his thoughts trying to conjure up what a two-humped camel looked like. "Anarani?" Laila tried to get his attention.

"Hmm?"

"Are you able to tell me about why you have those scars on your cheeks?" she asked again.

"Yes, yes. It is a story from a long time past and it began when I was very young. My father was still working with Ouhetta as a pack camel. As I told you, those camels have a more difficult nature than we riding camels. He was very strong-willed and fought the men and other camels, biting and kicking and spitting. I was not like him. I did what Ouhetta asked to get what I wanted. My mother protected me from my father, but the time came when I was separated from her. He fought with me, especially on the caravans. I think the word is "jealous," and my father got more jealous when he discovered me practicing the language of the people. That made him angrier, so he fought with me more. He kicked and used his teeth to bite my face. I was younger and strong, but my father was larger and fought very mean. The fights happened so often that Ouhetta knew he could not keep both of us. Of course, he kept me and sold my father."

"Oh, Anarani. That is so sad. Did you ever see him again?"

"The desert may be large, but where humans walk is well worn. I saw him in passing on caravans or in villages, but he never looked up to see me."

## THE REST OF THE STORY

Anarani did not want to tell Laila that he hated his father. He had the scars on his face to prove it, but he proudly wore those marks. They made him more determined than ever to make something of his unusual ability. He felt fated in his life, but for what he did not know.

What Anarani did have was a great fondness and respect for the man he carried on the caravans. Laila's father was gentle and accommodating to the conditions of the terrain they traversed. He would willingly dismount to make it easier for Anarani—lessening his burden over rough and steep areas. Anarani knew he wasn't from this land, not only by his language but also by how light he was in skin color.

There were times when they took shorter treks between villages. This was when a smaller female version of this man would be placed on his back to ride. He called her "Laila." Anarani particularly loved having her on his back because he would hear her delighted giggles spilling into his ears. As time passed during the trip, she would begin to hum a tune to the rhythm of his long-legged walk. There were no words; only his name filled the notes over and over to a sweet, lulling tune about her beloved Anarani. She sang it again and again.

He loved hearing it best after he sank down to his knees to allow her to dismount. She would then sing her song softly in his tufted ear while scratching his thickly furred, scarred cheek. It gently soothed and calmed his wandering heart and made his sandy eyelids heavy. Ever so gradually his long, crooked neck glided downward, longer and straighter until his chin touched the desert floor. It is said that when camels rest their heads on the ground they dream of fields of green grass.

"Where does she live now?" Anarani used to ponder as his daydreams of the girl melted away into the desert heat. The song's haunting melody would eventually disintegrate into the shoosh, shoosh, shoosh of the camels' pads landing on the sand. With a blink of his eyes, Anarani would once again become a camel in the caravan. It had been so many years since he carried her, but he took solace in knowing that he had once been a camel who had the joy of carrying the blue-eyed girl singing a lullaby in his ear.

## TEA

"I, the magical elixir of the Tuareg, am made through a tea maker's carefully measured alchemy of water, tea leaves, sugar, fire, and air. Tea makers must immerse themselves in my brewing. Making tea encompasses all the elements—earth to grow my leaves, water to brew them, fire to cook the water, and air to create the foam. And I simply must have a good head of foam. Brewing me to perfection means training in the precise techniques of steeping my leaves, adding the sugar, and pouring just the right amount of times for my foam. Yes, I am Tea and tea in the Sahara is a time-honored tradition of the Tuareg culture."

## BITTER LIKE LIFE

Ibrahim sat in a spot where he separated a portion of the burning logs from the main fire to make his tea. Next to him were his plastic shopping baskets that carried all of his tea brewing paraphernalia: three tea pots (two small and one slightly larger); two glass tumblers; twelve small glasses and their decorative, wooden holder; a package of green tea leaves; and a bag of sugar. All of these items were laid out around him. Once the tea making began, he performed all the steps to completion. Brewing was a hallmark of distinction and to honor his skill with no interruptions, the men did not ask his help with any other tasks.

Ibrahim flipped open the lid of the larger teapot that had been sitting on the fire, to assess the tea's readiness. Not finding it satisfactory just yet, he closed it, placed it back on the embers, waited a few more minutes, and then checked it again. Just before serving a round, he created foam by pouring the tea alternately between the large and small pots. Once in the small pot, Ibrahim repeatedly poured between the small pot and a glass, thus churning more air into the liquid.

As the group waited for their tea, Go'at pulled out his guitar. Stilted, yet rhythmical strains drifted over everyone. Laila kept hearing the fire's embers popping in time with the strange rhythm. It couldn't be her imagination. They were in synch too consistently, the fire taking on an echoing percussion, placing fiery emphasis on the syncopation. The men started singing as Ibrahim poured the tea back and forth between the pot and a glass—higher and higher, creating the foam and mixing the sugar. He tasted it, and when his refined taste buds registered just the right strength, he made his way around the circle to pour the first round. In order to swallow all of the foam, the tea drinker must slurp while drinking. Go'at and the others paused, drank their tea, and barely missing a beat, started up playing and singing again.

The bitterness of the tea pungently lingered in Laila's mouth. "Bitter like life," she thought to herself. Those words went 'round and 'round in her head as she sank deeper into the rhythm of the singing. The flickering light of the fire played tricks with the men's eyes. Laila gazed around to each veiled face. Their eyes seemed to reach out and hover in front of hers like the effect of a 3D movie. While their eyes stayed solid, their bodies became grainy and opaque, almost to the point of disappearing. One pair of eyes in particular locked with hers. They were Ouhetta's and they summoned her to follow, but not to actually get up and walk. Somehow she floated gently upward toward a field of pinpoint lights. Was she among the stars?

❁☼❁

Lighter and lighter, she felt her body disintegrating. The grains of her being filled the spaces between each point. Lightness, such lightness she felt, but this sensation didn't last very long. The graininess of her body then joined together and she found herself in a room. Her body was now intact though she knew she was not physically in the room as much as part of it.

The room was typical of Africa—sparsely furnished, this one with only a desk and two chairs. One chair was behind the desk and the other in front. The walls were of an adobe construction and one small high window cast a stream of strong sunlight onto the desk. There were two men in the chairs. As Laila's view joined with these environs, she suddenly realized that the man in the chair facing the desk was her father. Seeing him alive made her feel lightheaded, which seemed ironic for wasn't she already floating?

Her father appeared angry. This was very unfamiliar to her. She had never known her father to exhibit anything but wise patience to anyone he encountered. The other man was a gendarme who spoke with an authoritative air. His demeanor was feeding her father's anger. She could barely make out their words, which were in French. She tried to bring her attention to what was being said.

✺☼✺

However, in an instant she felt nothingness and awoke to the fire's glow. Go'at was once again supporting her with his arm around her shoulder. She still felt light and floating, not quite joined with her body. And as her awareness returned, words came flooding to the surface of her mind. She knew they must have come from the exchange she just witnessed, and they were not pleasant.

"*Du vas payer pour ça!*" (You will pay for this). The tone was angry and, without a doubt, spoken by the man across from her father.

Where had she gone and how had she gotten there? She surmised that she arrived somehow through her mind's eye. Or dare she believe that the sense of here and now contains the fingerprints of every preceding moment that ever led up to it? Is it possible that those fingerprints can be accessed when slipping into the interstices of time, space, and one's inner visions?

"Go'at?" Laila looked at him puzzling over where she had just been. "Where did I go? How did I see something that seemed so real, but that I have never experienced directly in my life?"

"Do you remember the conversation we had earlier this morning about embracing the unknown?" Laila nodded. "That is how you must be with these experiences. Where one journeys during the tea ceremony is not for rational explanation. I can only say that such an experience reflects how in tune you are within yourself and with all that is around you. Most people do not have the ability like you do to slip so quickly into the other spaces that open."

"Go'at, in these five days, I am realizing that there is so much more I must find out while I am here—not just about myself, but about my father's death. What can you tell me that might hold clues about why he was shot? Was it really just a stray bullet?"

"The only thing I can tell you is that he always tried to provide help to anyone who was struggling, even if it meant going against some of the restrictions laid down by the government. I advised him many times about the dangers a big heart could bring, but he would not listen."

Laila nodded and stared contemplatively at the fire. Ibrahim was making his way around the circle to pour the second round of tea. After he finished pouring Laila's, Go'at picked up the filled glass to hand to her. She gave Go'at a suspicious look, and hesitated.

"No, no, it's fine. Don't worry. The next rounds will not take you away," he reassured her. "Drink it in for some small comfort." The second round did not have the usual strength. She wondered if Ibrahim adjusted his brew so as to spare her any further visions.

The amount of information that was being revealed to her still held so many mysteries. Any memories of her father interacting with people, be they native to this area, as well as those in authority, were with diplomacy, but she realized how limited those memories were. There were many times when he traveled to other parts of the desert without her and her mother. What she observed in this vision was so real. She wanted to describe it to Go'at, but he and the other men were settling in to their evening with cajoling. Instead, she pulled out her journal to make notes and with that Ibrahim was standing at her glass pouring the third round.

As the fire died down, Laila with much exhaustion said her goodnights to the group. Go'at came over. "You have gone through a lot today, dear Laila. You should sleep well. But if not, or if you need anything, I will be camped out near the fire."

Laila nodded slowly, her eyes gazing blankly in the general direction he was pointing. He gave her a hug and she turned to head to her pad and sleeping bag tucked under a scrubby bush. Although she thought it would take her a while to settle down, once she slid in and her head touched the pillow, she easily slipped into sleep's lulling arms.

# THE WINDS OF REVOLUTION

In the late 1980s, the Tuareg who were still living a nomadic life roaming over borders laid down by expats, found themselves rounded up as refugees in Algeria. Various levels of negotiations were taking place as to where they belonged. An Islamic revolution to the north meant that area was too unstable for resettlement. As the UN weighed in on the negotiations, Niger finally accepted most of the refugees in 1990.

Although drought played a major role in the unrest of this time, political betrayals contributed to greater and greater distrust. But the distrust was mutual, as the Tuareg had the ancient reputation of raiding caravans and keeping slaves—especially black Africans. The Niger government, mostly composed of black Africans, was all too familiar with this reputation and planned to keep the refugees contained.

Jack was asked to help with settling these groups in the camp, given how long he had been studying their culture and the Tamasheq language. He would serve as a go-between with the Tuareg and the government authorities. Although he had experience working with encampments in Algeria, this was his first experience with a refugee camp. It meant leaving Katherine and Laila for a few months to take care of the situation. Jack would have Go'at accompany him to the camp then have him return. It took them four days to reach the camp. Jack knew that what lie ahead would require a level head, which would be a tall task given the heavy-handed military control.

✧✧✧

## A FIRSTHAND REPORT

The sun's rays began peaking over the horizon heralding the morning's dawn. Laila was dreaming of her mother and a powder puff she used to pat on her ears as a child. She would caress one ear then the other, so soft but ticklish at the same time. It would make Laila giggle. How real it seemed lingering in the foggy suspension of semi-consciousness, until she realized something actually was fondling her ear. Her eyes opened to discover a muzzle rubbing her head. She sat up and there was Anarani looking smugly at her.

"You are hard to wake," he barked in a whisper. Hearing this gruff voice coming from a camel, she thought another dream was about to begin.

"Come," he said, "follow me. If we talk here, they will hear us."

He sauntered away. Laila blinked several times to clear the sleep from her eyes and to watch this camel walking off with an apparent purpose to his stride. He paused, brought his neck around in a U-turn, and stared at her. Laila shook her head slightly, to further clear the cobwebs of sleep from her mind, then scrambled to dislodge herself from the twisted, bunched up sleeping bag. "Coming," she breathed as loudly as she could muster this early in the morning. Her dream had indeed ended. She crawled out into a chill that was driven by a stiff wind, so she grabbed her coat and *shesh*. Anarani was headed for a slight rise. Laila wrapped her *shesh* into sloppy layers, Baggee-style, as she stumbled to catch up with him. They continued in silence until Anarani stopped to survey the distance and the discreetness of where they stood.

"I think we should sit," he suggested. He went down on his front knees, followed by his back legs.

"I hope you don't mind," Laila said as she came over and huddled up against his shoulder. "It's cold and I could use a little protection from the wind." She crossed her arms for more warmth and asked, "So what is it you wanted to talk about?"

"I was standing near the fire last night and heard you talking. I believe you asked about the death of your father."

Any remnant of sleepiness bolted out of Laila's head. She sat up and swung around to face Anarani. The precariously tucked end of her *shesh* dislodged, letting the fabric unwind into her face. She fought to free herself from the tangle. "What can you tell me?" she asked now pulling the fabric into a pile around her shoulders. "Am I right to think that there was more behind my father's death than just a stray bullet?" Her voice was filled with uneasy anticipation.

✦✧✦

## THE WHISPERS OF REBELLION

Jack gave a final tug on the girdle of Anarani's saddle. Anarani moaned as most camels do when the belt is tightened under their belly, but it was more a perfunctory cry than from actual discomfort. He knew he could trust Jack to adjust the level of tautness to where it prevents the saddle from slipping, but not so far as to compromise his breathing and movements.

Anarani was surprised that he was being saddled this morning.

The caravan had just set up camp the prior day in a way that implied a longer stay. He and Go'at's camel were rounded up, along with two of the pack camels that were being loaded with water canisters and other supplies. Anarani gathered from Jack's words that they were to ride over the border to Niger. He knew the name where they were now was "Algeria," but he never understood what was meant by "border." It seemed to have something to do with stopping at a structure where there was a lot of paper exchanging and stamping, after which the ground where they walked took on a different name. But for the life of him, he could not understand; other than that small building, the landscape was wide open as far as one could see.

 Katherine and Laila were standing to the side watching while Jack saddled Anarani. Jack was telling them he would be back in a few months. He needed to help out with the resettlement of refugees at a camp in Niger. Once the saddle was on, Laila came over to Anarani and rubbed her head against his cheek. Anarani stopped chewing his cud and shook his head. He liked how Laila's hair tickled his cheek. She giggled and hugged his neck. "I'll miss you, Anarani," she said. Then she turned to her father. "I'll miss you, Daddy." Her arms went around his waist and he picked her up to give her a big hug. It was always sad to see her father leave, especially since it meant that her favorite camel had to go as well. The small caravan left, making its way due south. They were headed in the direction of the town Tchin-Tabaraden, near which was the refugee camp.

 On the fourth sunrise of their journey, Anarani saw the camp come into view. The tents were crowded together more than usual. He heard Jack tell Go'at that the authorities needed the refugees contained in a compact area to keep watch over them. Guards, patrolling with their guns at strategic locations, were the only form of boundary. Jack, Go'at, and their camels were escorted into the camp and led to the gendarme's tent, which was separate from the rest of the tents. Jack went in, telling Go'at to stay with the camels and to not yet let them loose to forage for food. Anarani tried to hear the voices inside, but they were talking very low. Jack came out in short order and spoke with the guard who pointed him in the direction of his tent, and nodded to Go'at to walk with him. Jack's tent stood closer to the refugee tents than the ones for the authorities. They walked with the camels and couched them at the opening of the tent, then went in. Anarani stopped chewing his cud so he could turn his ear to hear what he could of their conversation.

"Go'at, I am being placed in a very difficult position. This captain is asking me to be a spy on these people. I have been working among the Tuareg too many years to betray their trust, even these people with whom I have no familiarity."

"I advised you of this possibility," Go'at said with a tone that was uncharacteristically serious. "I am worried for you because the winds of rebellion are so strong now."

"I can't just up and leave." He paused. "Go'at, I'll be fine. Arrangements were made for me to be here that are too complicated to undo. Besides, I'm hoping that I can in some way alleviate the tensions building here."

"That is like carrying a camel on your back," Go'at euphemistically commented.

"I can't leave without trying. Besides, if it's a camel like Anarani he might be kind enough to slip off my back when the terrain gets too rocky and steep, don't you think?" They both laughed. Hearing these comments, Anarani pulled his head up from the lowered listening position, eyelids raised. Then he lowered his head again.

"You must leave in the morning to go back to our camp," Jack said. For now, let's get the camels out to forage, have some tea, and cook a little dinner. I have my concerns, but I only want you to tell Katherine that everything is going well when you return. I don't want her to worry any more than she may be already. She is well aware of what is brewing here. Any hint of unrest and her mind will go to the worst case scenario."

They got up and went out of the tent. Anarani sat chewing his cud and stood when the men gave their command to rise. Could he find ways to help Jack, given a camel is an equalizer that no one suspects? All it would take would be a few stealth movements in the dark along with his ability to understand human language.

Throughout the camp, whispers of rebellion circulated. The whispers floated into many ears including the gendarme in charge. It was his responsibility to find the culprits and place them under guarded surveillance apart from the larger camp population. Once Jack settled in at the camp, the gendarme had him escorted to his tent to discuss this topic.

"Have a seat," he said to Jack pointing to the only small, folding chair in front of the makeshift desk. His eyes were still focused on the paperwork that had covered the entire entourage at the border crossing between Algeria and Niger. Jack could tell from his dark skin and the way he spoke French that he was probably from Niger and educated in France, which also meant that he was from a well-to-do urban family. He had witnessed the degree of intolerance and prejudice displayed by such people toward the nomadic desert dwellers.

"I understand you are well-versed in the nomadic tribal culture and their tongue," the gendarme delivered in a flat tone while still perusing the paperwork.

"Yes," Jack responded in a similar flat tone.

"You are also aware," the gendarme raised his head for a focused delivery, "that there have been rumors of a possible rebellion within these groups?"

"No," Jack said with no particular emphasis. In truth, he did know. His gut told him to play it very cool. He knew he could extract more accurate information being among the people than from any military head.

"Consider yourself informed," he said giving Jack a suspicious look. As you work under my leadership, I will remind you that you are an agent of the Nigerien government. We have already accomplished a peaceful transport on our way to this camp. It is my intention to ensure and enforce good relations. I will count on your ability to work with these groups, keeping your ears and eyes open so no ill will stirs up the dust under our feet. Do I make myself clear?"

"Does that also mean I keep my ears and eyes open to ensure fairness and tolerance between those in charge of this mission and the people who rely on them for their safety and well-being?" Jack asked with his eyes looking squarely at the gendarme.

"That is already part of the equation," the gendarme responded in a measured tone while his eyes squinted into narrowed slits. "It will be in your best interest to work with me and report any activity that hints of retaliation. Am I understood?"

A strong wave of inner resistance rushed up Jack's spine hearing the gendarme's tone. It took every ounce of discipline not to stand up, voice his defiant words, and walk out. But he carefully weighed out the fact that his presence might help mitigate some of the tension. It brought to mind a Tuareg saying he learned: kiss the hand you cannot sever. This was going to be a role of playing to the authorities with delicate agreement while gaining the trust of the Tuareg they held.

"Quite," Jack answered the gendarme. He nodded his head knowing the curtain was already going up on a drama that could play out with serious consequences.

"Then I think we are done here. You may leave." He looked down at the pile of papers again and gave a small wave of his fingers.

Jack got up and walked out of the stifling atmosphere and gratefully breathed in the warm, evening air. To his left, he glanced a camel walking away in the shadows between the tents. He thought it looked familiar so he followed in its footsteps. As he got closer, his hunch was right; it was Anarani. He said his name, and Anarani stopped.

"What's up, boy?" he said rubbing Anarani's scarred cheeks. He led him along, and when they reached his tent, Jack couched him. He went in and brought out some grain he had as a supplement to whatever scarce food was available. Jack squatted next to Anarani who munched through the pile of food. He gazed over the camp contemplating his next steps, but he didn't want to get too far ahead of himself. For now, it would be one day at a time getting to know who this community was and what they were thinking. With his years of studying the Tuareg, he knew it wouldn't take long to gain their trust.

Jack worked quickly to put his community connections into place. He was soon able to approach the camp elders. Introduction by way of connections allowed their conversations to be less formal, more direct. When he brought up the developing rebellion, the elders were initially reticent to speak of any specific knowledge. "Here, in these conditions, we are all rebels," was their general sentiment.

And, to add to the rebellious atmosphere, the conditions within the camp were not good. They were born of desperation from the government marginalizing the Tuareg groups. Relying on sustenance from the very authorities who were enforcing harsh measures inside as well as outside of the camp amplified their vulnerability, leading disgruntled youth within the camp to resort to an equally harsh response through words of retaliation.

Jack found as much time as he could to sit with the Tuareg in order to gain their trust. He cultivated a rapport with a few key informants who held him in their confidence. They conveyed the messages of the rebellious whispers. He tried to explain the futility of such an action, given the disadvantages refugees have in relation to the controlling authorities. But what could one man do? He didn't want to betray the trust of those confiding in him by taking his knowledge to the authorities. He knew they would only squelch it with a heavy hand. He learned of three very vocal young men whose words rang out protesting the difficulties of the camp. They had little food or shelter from the corrupt siphoning of supplies. Again, he tried to reason with their retaliatory tone and even went to those in charge to increase the volume of food delivered, but his words were lost to the atmosphere of power and control. The injustice was feeding their rebellious plans not their empty stomachs.

One night Jack was awakened to a hand shaking his shoulder. It was Shikou, one of his informers. He looked nervous and agitated. He came to ask a favor of Jack. It was related to their plans to institute justice, or at the very least to put those enforcing injustice in their place. They needed weapons to force this cause. Jack heard him out and it was not an easy place to be ensnared. He, being a part of the faction overseeing the camp, would be less suspect and could help those living under the majority's rule to access the means by which to shake up their choking grip. In other words, Jack could be a crucial leg of their arms acquisition.

## WIND

"In a landscape of exaggerated shadows, infinite stars and sand, massive massifs, and scattered lone acacia trees, nothing, not even human habitation can fill the desert space. This void is best filled by my presence. I am wind: the most flowing force, save water. One learns quickly in the desert that there is plenty of wind and plenty of thirst. And it is by my fancy whether or not you welcome, or shrink, from my power."

# THE HERDER OF THE DESERT

From the first day Laila joined the caravan, the wind made its presence known. But this morning the wind went from a benign tap on the shoulder to the demanding orders of a drill sergeant. It dictated Laila's attention constantly. Such conditions bring any Westerner to greater appreciation for the adaptive use of the *shesh*. Those yards and yards of fabric around the head serve as warmth and a barrier to the wind's penetrating effects, as well as to protect the face from pelting sand. Laila's sunglasses masked the only area left exposed.

The usual crisp, defined edges of the landscape blurred to a hazy suspension of sand. Even the sun's brightness was dulled, though not a cloud floated by. The conditions produced the same sensation as wanting to wipe the crust from the eyes to clear one's vision in the morning. But the crust hung in the air, not in the eyes. It made for weary traveling. If there was one thing Laila hated, it was moving through a forceful, bitter wind. All she could do was curl in on herself for warmth and protection. As slow as the pace of a caravan can be, such a strength of velocity slowed them down further.

The wind drove Laila deeper within, not being able to focus on the surrounding scenery. Here she was journeying back to the very place she last remembered her father and he could very well be passing over her literally as particles in the wind.

"C'mon, Laila," she thought to herself. "It's been twenty years and many sandstorms since then. How could his ashes not have dispersed miles and miles away by now?" She wasn't quite sure whether she felt comfort thinking of his ashes blowing over her or of his ashes so long lost.

She tried to disengage from her disquieting thoughts, but the day's unsettling ride was stirring up much along with that morning's exchange with Anarani. It was the first real clue to what may have happened to her father. That he had walked a very fine line between the authorities and the Tuareg people had been a very dangerous choice. Anarani's disclosure of what Jack was confronted with when he went to the refugee camp did shed some light, but there was more to learn. They couldn't talk for long that morning as Go'at noticed that Laila was not nearby and made his way to find her. But it was enough information for now.

Laila patted Anarani's haunches grateful not only for his presence, which was steeped in comfort from years ago, but also for his unexpected and inconceivable gift of speech. Everything felt surreal as they moved slowly on in the wind's steady strength. That is the gift of the desert; giving up what one considers "real" for the desert is filled with interstices. Between the wind, shadows, rocks, boulders, sand, and scattered flora, dwell innumerable spaces. These are where magic arises, pushing the edges of perception and expectation. Only by opening one's mind and heart can magic be accessed. Laila sat back in the saddle feeling the warmth of her own breath within the veil as the breath of the wind blew all around her. Her defenses were waning and she was giving in to the haziness of the conditions, both inner and outer.

※※※

The caravan reached a point where the sandy desert became littered with varying sized rocks. The flat terrain gave way to slanted, rocky passages. These conditions, along with the harsher wind, were difficult at best. The caravan had to make its way down a rocky hill between tall boulders. However, the angle of the incline was not so steep as to prohibit riding. Go'at, Ibrahim, and Laila remained seated, while the walking scouts, Ouhetta and Baggee, guided the pack camels.

Midway down the hill, Anarani suddenly stopped in his tracks surprising Laila and the camels behind him. Simultaneously, and in one fell swoop, Ouhetta was nimbly running to his side. In seconds, Laila felt herself falling into Ouhetta's waiting arms, then gently placed on the ground as her saddle slipped sideways. Ouhetta immediately grabbed the saddle to right it. A knot had loosened from the increased angle and more pronounced movements of Anarani's shoulders. With keen Tuareg vigilance, tuned in to all that is around them, a disaster was averted: Laila falling from the height of a camel's shoulders.

Ouhetta retied the twine. The other nomads came to Laila to make sure she was alright. She felt quite fussed over while reassuring them that she was intact. They decided that she proceed walking with Anarani in tow just to make sure no further mishaps took place. The caravan had no sooner begun to move when to Laila's embarrassment, she felt the pants of her *gandora* give way and fall down. The drawstring had also loosened. Again there was an abrupt stop while Laila stooped down to quickly pull up her pants. But her *shesh* went askew, so she couldn't see what she was doing. There she was trying to right the pile of material on her head while reaching for the pile of material around her ankles. The image in her head of doing this made her start laughing so hard she almost toppled forward from the angle. This set all of the nomads into hearty, infectious laughter, which lasted quite a number of minutes. Luckily, Laila had long johns on underneath, and the length of the *gandora* covered down to below her knees. When she finally tied her pants and Baggee helped rearrange her *shesh*, the caravan continued on its way. Laila looked up at Anarani. He had a look of amusement twinkling in his eyes, as he rubbed his snout on her Baggee-wrapped head.

◎☼◎

Toward the end of the day, and luckily by the time they stopped for the night, relief came as the wind's strength weakened. Sitting by the campfire, Laila brought up her discomfort about the intensity of the wind.

"Ahh," said Ibrahim in his deep, bass voice. "There is a Tuareg saying: 'When the wind blows, the desert trembles.' And the effects of the trembling are not just felt by man and beast, but by the dunes and every grain of sand. We are lucky that today we did not encounter the even stronger *harmattan*. Had this been the *harmattan* we would have stopped the caravan, its force is so harsh." Laila shuddered to think of sitting in a greater velocity of wind, especially with no cove or large rocks to provide any protection. Ibrahim continued.

"The wind is the great herder of the desert. The sand grains, whether they are part of the dunes—large and solitary, or small and clustered—the flat expanses, or even part of the massifs, are the flock of the wind."

"We are herders ourselves," said Baggee. "So we have much respect for the wind who can move so large a flock. When the wind blows, the grains of sand must obey."

"We will tell you a story about why we live as nomads," Ouhetta chimed in as he stirred the cooking pot on the fire. "There are days when wind is gentle. He enjoys a rest and soaks up the intense heat of the sun. He blows just enough to pet his flock of dunes and all the grains of sand. He is content seeing them respond to his whispers—spiraling, dancing, swirling—then settling back down. The wind takes great pride in his handiwork as he herds his flock into chiseled crests and symmetrical ripples perfectly aligned with each other. The dunes and sand may stretch hundreds of miles, but the wind oversees them all as far as the eye can see. It is the nature of wind to be everywhere."

"It is also the nature of wind to be fickle, becoming bored in an instant," Baggee continued. "When he tires of the settled features, he may feel the urge to mix things up. And so the dunes and sand never know when his force will rise. With one big breath he blows the order into chaos. With invisible arms he scoops up thousands of grains and carries them tirelessly not just through the familiar features of the blue sky above them, but to mythic distances never to be seen again. The dunes shape-shift in response to the wind, swallowing up objects and even whole towns in their path."

"And so," Ibrahim concluded, "the very life of dunes and all the sand they are composed of are destined to be nomadic, ready to be herded to the next location according to the wind's whim. No dune, no sand grain can live a sedentary life. Thus is the nature of the trembling desert. To be a people of the desert who dare dwell in such conditions, we must also follow the ways dictated by the wind and the sand. The desert may be sparse of life, but it is always on the move."

Laila let the beautiful story wash over her and looked up at the billions of stars suspended in the dark night sky. She again wondered about how far her father's ashes may have traveled. He loved learning about cultures and had traveled so much of the world before becoming an anthropologist. His request to remain here meant he could be part of a place and people to which he had become deeply connected. But it also allowed him to carry on as a mythic nomad of the world.

# THE DUNES

"We, in ceaseless dialogue with the wind, are tirelessly shape-shifting, enduring endless transformations. Even when our dialogue is a mere whisper, impermanence lingers in the air. We succumb to shedding our layers like a snake; our grains of sand take wing like a bird. Our movements may be barely perceptible;

but one minute we are here, the next where you are trying to force the futile hand of permanence. No say have we. Although our heights may outweigh the wind in size, we are only composed of the lightest of particles. When they are whisked up in grand proportions, the sun disappears, as do we, eventually. Yes, we are truly the teachers of impermanence so learn from us and live always on the whim of your heart's desire."

# STRONG LIKE LOVE

The next evening, as the men unloaded the camels and set up the campsite, Laila let Go'at know she wanted to wander off into one of the branching valleys for a walk. He made sure she was outfitted with the essential desert gear—a container filled with water, a flashlight, and a whistle. With her well-being in check, she entered a passage made up of a wide expanse of sand bordered by tall, vertical rock walls. Large boulders were strewn about, some chaotically piled against the sides of the high rock faces. An occasional scrubby bush or clump of grass was interspersed among the sand, rocks, and boulders.

It felt good to go into a quiet space with all that was being revealed on this journey. She ventured out as she would when she entered the woods back home, paying close attention to her body's inner sensations and the surroundings in order to see what would beckon.

Laila used the technique of letting herself go wherever she felt drawn, whether by an inner sensation, a bird or plant that caught her eye, or even a patch of dappled sunlight. She took them as signs to find a niche in which to nestle, to allow a wisdom greater than her years to fill her. She couldn't explain the wise voice or its origin, but it came only when she let go of what she called her "surface voices." When she quieted her mind by listening intently to nature speaking around her, and focused on some matter about which she needed clarity, she often felt like a dawn breeze was rustling up whatever was hidden within.

Sinking deeper into her awareness, Laila closed her eyes, took a deep breath, and stood quietly listening to the rhythm of her breathing and heartbeat. Then she began to focus on the outer world, which today held only a whisper of the wind. She began to take slow and mindful steps, her eyes gazing down as each foot created a depression. When thoughts arose, she envisioned them being swallowed up by the grains of sand, emptying her mind and opening her heart.

In the Sahara, emptiness is vast—much like the feeling of emptiness inside when someone leaves us. And when we have deeply loved that someone, it stirs up nostalgia. With nostalgia comes longing and, like a melody written in the expressiveness of a minor key, the feelings it evokes can bridge one heart to another. The call of the desert and the longing within Laila's heart were one and the same, for they both held the loss of her father. Laila walked hoping that she could tap into an expansiveness that was larger than her, into that infinite space of the desert that holds mysteries beyond our powers of perception.

Laila continued on the side of the canyon still steeped in the late day sun, following the edges of the shadows as they swallowed up the light. Making her way toward a large boulder, her eyes caught something sticking up slightly in the sand. She reached down and dislodged a small, black horn with a bit of white skull still attached. It had belonged to a gazelle; and perhaps near where there was one, its match might also be found. Looking around the immediate area and moving the sand with her feet, she indeed found a second horn. This was an unusual and exciting find.

She sat down on a boulder to inspect them more closely. "What had happened to this gazelle?" Laila thought. "What predator had been here, or had the gazelle become weak and died on its own?" From the teachings her parents had given her about the wildlife of the Sahara, her guess was that this was a Dorcas gazelle. The horns were very slender. Around the thicker part of the shaft were many rows of evenly spaced raised rings, which gave way to a smooth surface up to the tips. Laila wanted to contemplate this find in her journal but when she started to pull it out, she heard something approaching. It was just on the other side of the craggy cove she was tucked into.

Her heart started to beat, perhaps from letting her mind ponder this creature's ultimate demise and the fact that dusk is when predators start to emerge. She felt frozen on the boulder, not wanting to be heard, all the while hearing the footsteps getting closer. They were nearing the curve around which she sat. That was when the horns took on a look of a dagger. She turned them with pointed tips sticking out, one in each hand. Barely breathing, she readied herself and what rounded her view was…Anarani.

They stared at each other: Anarani casually standing, chewing his cud and Laila poised with two gazelle horns raised in her hands. Without skipping a beat, Anarani quirked, "And why in the name of Allah are you challenging me to a fight?"

Laila brought her hands down exhaling. "Anarani, you nearly scared me to death."

He glumly chewed his cud and walked toward her.

"And don't give me that one brow down look of sarcasm either," Laila admonished him.

"What is this 'sarcasm' word?"

Laila chuckled, for he was the new definition of sarcasm in her mind. "It's just, well, you being you." She reached out to give him a hug around the base of his neck. "Look what I found!" She again held up the horns.

"Yes, yes, an *aschenked*."

"Oh, right, gazelle in Tamasheq. It's quite a find. And if I had found addax antelope horns, that would have been even more amazing. They're really rare."

"Maybe, but I have seen them deeper in the mountains."

"What other creatures have you seen? I remember seeing little jerboas when I was a child. I think that's *edaoui* in Tamasheq. They look like jumping mice. So cute."

"I suppose. Hmmm, when I am out with the other camels at night, I see *ezzuguzz*."

"Let me see, *ezzuguzz* is fennec fox? And *aghardum* always scared me."

"What is *aghardum* in your language?"

"Scorpion."

"Laila!" Go'at was calling down the canyon. It was time to eat.

"Yes, coming!" she called back. They both turned toward the camp and started walking. Laila looked up at this most magical beast, his cheeks with their scars, and the story about them. Laila patted his cheek and placed her hand on his shoulder as they walked. At the threshold of the canyon, he nuzzled the side of her *shesh* and walked the opposite direction. Laila watched him, thinking how normal he looked in that moment, then made her way to the nomads.

As usual, this was the time of day when the men were animated and chatting, each contributing their part in preparing the evening meal. Laila loved watching their interactions. Unlike men in the Western world, there was a closeness that they exhibited by sometimes holding hands while they walked in the caravan. It was the kind of hand holding that conveyed a sense of reassurance that they were there for each other living in such a harsh environment. When gathered around the campfire, they laughed and cajoled with gusto and could end up like a puppy pile all flopped close and even on top of each other. A sense of humor enveloped them in a cloak of comfort and playfulness, especially sitting in the darkness of night.

As everyone sat down to have their meal, Laila showed the men her find. "Ahh," said Ibrahim nodding his head knowingly, "you have found your vulnerability."

"What do you mean?" Laila asked.

"*Aschenked* must live always alert. The herd is protection, but if separated—that is when their vulnerability brings danger. We nomads must also be part of a group to survive, especially in such a vast desert. If we separate to walk another path, there must always be a place to fill our bags with water and our stomachs with food, and most importantly, our hearts with connections. As a saying goes, 'What I wish best for myself, I wish it for my friends too.'"

"I am very lucky," Laila said as she looked at each of the men. "To be here again getting closer to where my father died could not have happened without you. Hearing your wise words and feeling your guidance gives me the courage to continue on, and I thank each of you for being with me."

"Laila," Go'at looked at her, "we hold great respect for your mother and father. They certainly passed on a deep commitment to following your heart, as they followed theirs. We are honored that we can walk with you." Laila could not say anything. Her eyes teared up from the memories, while she smiled to show her gratitude for how held she felt in this group.

After their meal and cleaning up, the group resettled around the fire while Ibrahim passed out the first round of tea. Ibrahim began a low, breathy hum. The others sang softly. When it was time for the second round of tea, strong like love, the tea's effect and the men's chanting seeped into Laila's awareness. When her eyes closed, there was a sensation of being transported.

To her surprise, she was again standing in the exact place where she had looked down and seen one gazelle horn, then the other, partially revealed in the sand. In this vision, she spied a gazelle leaping and prancing playfully a short distance away. She hoped the creature would not be startled as she observed the apparent joy it exhibited. Laila couldn't help but share in the joy and lightness of its being. Her heart had never felt anything quite like this before, and just at that moment the gazelle stopped and fixed its eyes intently on her. With lithe, graceful steps it started to walk in her direction. Then it stopped.

Gazelle's eyes were like deep ancient wells of wisdom, as dark as tar, as liquid as water, soft and inviting. They beckoned Laila. With the intensity of the gazelle's gaze, Laila fell under its spell and she obeyed. As she approached, she extended her hand slightly, palm side up. The gazelle gently nuzzled Laila's hand then stood back. Their eyes met again. Deeper still, the two round pools—whose dimensions seemed boundless—drew her in. Laila entered a space of suspended awareness, a dream world embedded in the one she had already entered. She felt her longings rush through her blood, filling the chambers of her heart. It pounded within her chest and her whole body seemed to vibrate. She then heard an endearing female voice fill her head.

"Are you willing to listen with the ears of your heart to all the voices of yourself speaking?" Laila recalled a wise voice such as this from her quiet rests in nature back home. This time the voice seemed to come from the being standing in front of her.

"Who are you?" she asked, but she was still not sure if she was questioning the voice in her head, the gazelle, or if they were one and the same.

"I am Aschenked," the gazelle answered. "I am the joy that leaps in your heart. I am the strength that helps you to endure the path to your heart's desire." As she spoke, Aschenked walked slowly around Laila.

"Why have you come to me?" Laila lifted her hand gently towards the gazelle as it approached her. Aschenked playfully maneuvered her nose into Laila's palm and licked it.

Without pretense or pause, Aschenked began to speak as she circled Laila. "Life is precarious as an *aschenked*—avoiding predators, searching for scarce food and water, protecting our young. We must always live in the moment, alert, with instincts heightened to our surroundings. We survive not only by our individual senses, but also by connecting communally. There is strength in numbers as we pay close attention to all the messages passed among the herd, the vibrations of each single heartbeat linking one to another." Aschenked continued her slow walk around Laila. She faced her once again and gazed into Laila's eyes. Laila stood entranced, unable to move, with no words to offer.

"Following your heart's desires requires you to live like the *aschenked*—with heightened awareness about the precarious nature of life. It compels you toward the darkened chambers of your heart. Opening the chamber doors, confronting the pain and grief that lies within, releasing the patterns of protection that helped you to survive life's bitterness, can fill you with fear and doubt. Most avoid dealing with the hurt and vulnerability this brings, especially since it does not guarantee life will be any easier. Delving into your own darkness and void is like glimpsing into the darkness that all humans carry." Aschenked yet again paced around Laila. An energetic, tingly sensation passed over her skin each time the gazelle circled.

"Choosing such a path brings healing and expands the capacity for love, not only for yourself but for others as well. The clarity that comes allows you to see things in ways that others do not understand. Just as each *aschenked* must convey its message to the herd to help keep it strong, so it is important to share the vibrations and messages of your heart with others to build strength in your community." Aschenked stood in front of Laila and asked, "Will you take my words to heart?" Laila still could not find her voice, so she nodded her response.

Then she spoke her final message, "Love is only as strong as the heart from which it radiates. The more open your heart, the stronger love will grow and thrive. One heart opens another heart. If a heart doesn't open another heart, life is not worth living."

And with these words, the air between them filled with silky, shimmering threads, radiating between their hearts, connecting beast to human. Aschenked backed away from Laila. Her form continued to fade into the distance until she and the emanating threads disintegrated. Laila felt a blanket of darkness envelop her.

Next thing she knew she was again with the nomads wrapped in a camel blanket lying on the ground next to the campfire.

# RITE OF PASSAGE: STAGE II

# THRESHOLD

(Testing the soul, learning lessons, awaiting rebirth)

## LAILA'S JOURNAL ENTRY

I am stepping back and forth across thresholds, between worlds. How many worlds, I do not know. But these visions and their stories are letting me know the world is layered and intricate. The world as I once defined it is being challenged. In this vast desert at night, the darkness allows me to observe millions of galaxies above. And I ask: are there millions more in the multitude of sand below our feet, the interstices of our minds, or even the interstitial connections of our hearts? Where does one heart end and another begin? But the senses live where they live and will only expand if you quiet your mind. I feel my senses expanding around, among, and between thresholds I am only beginning to glimpse.

## INNER AND OUTER ALLIES

When the caravan finally reached the oasis, many days had passed and Laila's sense of linear time was all but lost. Yet there seemed to be nothing but time in the desert; days undulated one to another like dunes over the horizon. Each moment was measured in transient footprints, stirred and swallowed up by wind and sand. Such a landscape makes every footstep feel pregnant with promise that one will arrive someplace— and one must arrive in the desert, else your life expires.

And so they came to this thriving spot to replenish their supply of water and rest the camels for a day before leaving for the village. Since a variety of other people were also taking respite here, the men put up two tents: one to place the food and other items they traveled with, and another to give Laila some privacy. Once the flurry of activities to settle in subsided, Laila took the opportunity to sit within the shaded coolness of her tent to contemplate this incredible journey and all the mystical happenings that were stirring the depths of her soul. She closed her eyes and sat in meditative stillness. Within the quiet of this space and her mind, she conjured up the myriad images and experiences from the last few weeks on caravan. They drifted by like clouds, each raining their droplets of wisdom upon her.

Taking a deep breath, Laila felt a tingling sensation rise up in the pit of her stomach. It was not the uncertainty or fear that came before she left, but a feeling of strength that she had not experienced for as long as she could remember. Sinking into the intense connections with the Tuareg, their tea ceremony, the desert, Anarani, and all the visions, she couldn't help but feel a desire to go off on her own, away from the comfort of the caravan. With all the clues and insights the journey had revealed to her, she felt ready to face the final stretch toward the place where the ill-fated event had torn her father from her.

It was time to ally with all the parts of herself that were waking up: the little girl who lost her innocence with the loss of her father, the teenager who never felt like she fit in, and the young adult who was restless within the void of her heart. They had long been a part of her, but Laila was gaining an awareness of each of them and the gifts their struggles brought to her life. She felt even more emboldened to pursue her desire to venture out on her own, given the companionship and guidance of Anarani. He would know where the village was located, given his years of travel to and from that area. Of course, that particular detail would be difficult to disclose while expressing her conviction to Go'at. She knew that Anarani was very careful about not being found out; but then, who was more trustworthy than Go'at? She simply must ask Anarani if he would make himself known to Go'at. There wouldn't be any harm in asking.

Laila left her tent to find the camels. She blinked from the brightness of the sun held up by the deep azure blue sky, cloudless as usual. Surveying the oasis, she saw some of the camels resting in the most amusing manner. Four of them had sunk down behind a bush so that only their heads popped out on top. A few others were standing in the spaces between. All were staring off looking cool and collected while chewing their cud. Anarani was not among them, so she walked in another direction to see if he might still be grazing in the trees just beyond. Then she spied him with his neck lowered sucking down a long drink from the watering trough.

"Anarani," she whispered as loud as she could in her approach. He looked up. "Can we go somewhere to talk?"

He surveyed the area from his vantage point and decided on a direction they should take. Their eyes met and Laila knew to follow. They walked a distance that brought them to the edge of the oasis, yet still with foliage that would screen them as they sat. "And what is it you want to talk about?" Anarani asked.

"It's about going the rest of the way to the village. Do you know your way there on your own?"

"It is a path I know from my many years on caravan, yes."

"It's kind of hard to explain, but I would like to go there, just the two of us without Go'at and the others. I want to face this difficult part of my quest on my own."

"Hmmmm. And do you think Go'at will grant you such a wish?"

"Well, that depends…," she leaned in and whispered in his ear as she rubbed it, "on you."

He enjoyed the rub for mere seconds, until he thought better of her words. "What do you mean it depends on me?" He turned his long snout so quickly it bumped Laila's head and almost knocked her over.

She righted herself, and continued. "If Go'at knew that you are as aware as you are, then…"

"My dear girl!" he interrupted her. "Are you saying that I show him I am a camel who talks and understands people?"

"But Go'at is very trustworthy and I'm sure he could keep it a secret!" she said emphatically.

"I only shared this with you because you are not from here. The men are very close and do not keep secrets from each other, trustworthy or not."

Laila thought. She did not want to compromise his delicate position, but she wanted to break free, feel the growing expansion, and exercise an intelligence she had never known before. So with great care, she spoke. "You said you felt fated about your gift, right?" Anarani nodded. "Well, I have come here and you have revealed this gift to me. No harm has come yet to you has it?"

"No, but I trust you."

"I know. And do you feel that you are already on a path that is taking you closer to delivering this gift in ways that help?"

"I am helping you, am I not?"

"Yes, very much so. And I'm asking you to keep trusting what I'm asking and to use even more this magical skill that has taken you many years to learn."

❁❁❁

# A WITNESS

With the relocation of the refugees to the town of Tchin-Tabaraden, Jack was becoming more and more suspicious of this

Nigerien government resettlement program. The goods that were promised these people, including food and tents, were not adequate and were, by all accounts, being sold by corrupt government officials. His interactions with the gendarme overseeing this camp fed his suspicions. When he was granted an audience with him so he could convey the deprivations in the camp, the captain would take down his requests and suggestions begrudgingly enough showing that he had very little interest in the welfare of the refugees.

Jack's years of living with the Tuareg and sinking into their culture meant he felt a deep allegiance to their struggles. He had witnessed all that the droughts, economic crisis, and political oppression had placed on this region and the people, given his travels had begun long before he became an anthropologist. His interests and devotion fed his anthropological training. Now that he had many more years of study, he was not surprised at the brewing insurrection.

On the caravan to Tchin-Tabaraden, Jack offered a ride on Anarani to a pregnant woman and a frail elderly lady while he walked along with the rest of the refugees. Some of the guards walked, but the head gendarme and other guards rode camels. Jack tried to reason with the guards who had riding camels to provide them for the vulnerable individuals, but they were under orders to ride. Jack did not even attempt to argue, as his diplomatic position was rapidly wearing down to a one-sidedness and opinions that the captain did not welcome.

Jack was made privy to covert conversations among the refugees. They positioned themselves as much out of earshot of the guards as they could. Of course, in a caravan the captain and guards riding on their camels could still see Jack talking among the refugees. Jack could not keep playing the game that went so against his heart and conscience. He knew the Tuareg at least needed a person to witness their pain, even if he was powerless to relieve it.

## AN "INNOCENT" BYSTANDER

At the highest heat of the day, the caravan came to a rest. There was little shade for the refugees, but being a resourceful people familiar with scarcity, the men utilized their *sheshes* and the women, their veils, to create small patches in which to sit protected from the sun. The camels were gathered around the only acacia tree picking at the thorny branches, under which sat the captain and his men. This group was also having its own covert conversation. Anarani was happy to have the excuse of the tree to give him full listening capacity.

"So our diplomat is sitting over there eating with the refugees," observed the captain to his next-in-command. "I see him talking with them as we walk. Have you overheard any of their conversations?" he asked.

"No, sir. As I make my way closer to where I see a group talking with him, they disperse, but as I reported back at the camp, there are whispers of men trying to access arms."

"Yes, and what better way to set that up than with an expat. I do not trust that man. He is feeding their thoughts of rebellion in more ways than just sentiments," implied the captain. "Once we get these refugees secure and he goes back to his part of the desert, let's take care of this issue. We will know when the time is right and there will be no association to our actions."

Anarani had been standing stock still throughout the whole exchange so he could hear, and with that last statement, he gulped his cud too quickly, which made him cough a very loud camel cough. Out came the cud in direct line of the captain's head. He shot up, flailing his arms to get it off, catching everyone's attention—his men and the refugees. No one dared laugh out loud. His men came to his assistance while he was on the verge of pulling out his pistol. But thinking better of it, all he did was curse Anarani telling the men to get that horrid beast away from him. Jack was running over when he heard the shouting, and led Anarani away. From that point in the journey, Jack kept Anarani close. He was looking forward to the end of this unpleasant task.

## FOR LOVE AND RESPECT

Anarani sat in silence after Laila's request to trust her about revealing his ability to speak. Laila wanted to say more but thought better of it, allowing the silence to linger. He looked off in a most pensive manner not even chewing his cud. Laila knew this request was bothering him, which didn't surprise her at all. The sounds from the oasis filled the moments, while the brightness of the day transitioned into the soft glow of dusk.

Finally, Laila quietly said, "Anarani?"

"Yes, Laila I am here," he reassured her. With a heavy breath, he began to talk. "Laila, I have something to tell you that is not easy. It is about your father." He paused. Laila sat waiting. "Just before the rebellion, your father helped move people to another place. The gendarmes in charge were not kind to these people and Jack tried to help make things better for them. Those in command did not like Jack, so much so that I heard them talk about harming him. I wanted to tell him, but I was young and still very uncertain about showing anyone I could talk, even your father."

"What are you saying?"

"When your father was shot that day in the village, you and your mother and the Tuareg were not the only ones who lost someone you loved. I lost my master who I carried and who was always kind and gentle to me as well as to everyone. Since that day, I wondered…if I had said something to him, would he have been more on guard, or left sooner?"

"So do you think it was not a random attack or a stray bullet?" Laila asked.

"I cannot say for sure, but I lost a chance to warn him because I was too afraid to speak. I do not want to lose another chance to help someone I love," he said nudging Laila's *sheshed* head. She giggled as she rearranged it.

"Does this mean that you will let Go'at hear who you are?"

"Yes, Laila, if it means that much to you. But only to him." His brows went down, making him look very serious. "There is such a thing as *ashek*, the Tuareg honor code, and I know this will hold his trust."

"Oh, thank you, Anarani!" She started rubbing his ear and humming his song. He tried not to enjoy it, but how relaxed she made him feel. His neck went slightly forward and down, down, down went his chin to the ground. He remembered how he had dreams of Laila and in them she would offer him delicious, moist flowers. Over the years, he had longed to see her smile, smell her sweet hair, and hear the lullaby that brought him peace and contentment. She appeared in his dreams along with her father, and now she was here and it was the least he could do to grant her request out of love and respect for them both.

## ONE REBELLIOUS ACTION...
## AND ANOTHER

Only days after the refugees were resettled in the town of Tchin-Tabaraden, an unfortunate occurrence took place that was to fuel the revolution, along with the subsequent squelching of it by government authorities. An armed attack led by a Tuareg political opposition group took place on a prison compound. Some of the disgruntled young men from the relocated refugees joined this rebellion. It was a call to action that channeled their anger fed by the unfair treatment they had just experienced. Some of the gendarmes, and many of the rebels, were killed. Even with the loss of life, those who survived managed to steal weapons. They had resorted to violence in order to be heard. Jack was already heading back the day before the prison incident took place.

This escalated the Nigerien government's anger and, as a result, they sent in soldiers to find the guilty men. Unable to do so, later that same month they went on a rampage: torturing, arresting, and killing a large number of innocent Tuareg civilians. Only days after the rampage had begun in Tchin-Tabaraden, the skirmish that led to Jack's death took place.

## ANARANI REVEALED

When Laila returned to their camp in the oasis, she found Go'at and the others sitting ready for Ibrahim to start the rounds of tea.

"Ahh, Laila, come join us for tea," he said as he gestured for her to sit in the group. Laila came over and sat next to Go'at. "I take it you are settled in your tent?"

"Yes, but I think I prefer to sleep outside of it. After all, there is no better view to fall asleep to than the desert sky."

"I agree. And you have acquainted yourself with the oasis?"

"Not too much. Mostly over there toward the edge," she pointed in the direction where she and Anarani had been sitting." Go'at nodded.

Ibrahim walked around pouring tea in the glasses sitting in front of each person. All the men were particularly quiet and not in their usual joviality. Maybe it was the fact that there were more people around them. They were not cloaked by the surrounding vastness of the desert and, thus, were on their best behavior. Laila sat pensively staring into the fire. She wanted to talk to Go'at, but not with the others so close. She decided to wait until the last round of tea and hoped that there would be no visionary interventions along the way.

Her wish was granted as they slurped down the second and third rounds, unceremoniously. They ate dinner, still with very little talk. And as they settled around the evening's fire, Laila was becoming quite tired. But she was anxious to broach this topic before morning. As she got up and said her goodnights, she asked Go'at if she could talk with him.

"Yes, Laila, what is it? You seem very distant tonight, although I think we are all feeling this journey's effect on us."

"Go'at, I need you to come with me so I can show you something." She motioned for him to follow and turned. They walked in silence to where she and Anarani had been sitting. Laila called Anarani's name. Within minutes, they heard the shoosh, shoosh, shoosh of his approach. Laila looked at him hoping to get some glimmer of recognition, but he merely stood chewing his cud as any normal camel would do. He couched himself and Laila indicated that Go'at sit in front of Anarani. Go'at gave him a rub on his nose and sat down. Laila sat to the side of both of them.

"I guess you are wondering why I brought you to sit with Anarani," she said looking at Go'at. Then she glanced down, hesitating before she continued. "I have something to ask of you, a permission that sort of depends on Anarani." Go'at sat quietly with a puzzled look on his face. "I would like to go the rest of the way to the village on my own."

Go'at looked at Laila, then he looked down for a moment. When he looked up again he said, "Laila, it is one thing to go into the desert led by nomads who have known this way of life for thousands of years, but you have only been back a few weeks. For you to venture into unknown territory…" he shook his head, "I have too many concerns. And what reasons do you have to go without the caravan? Even we nomads rarely travel without companionship."

"But companionship is exactly what I would have. What if I could go with a very knowledgeable ally, one who not only knows the direction but also the ways of the desert and the people?"

"I do not understand. How could that be without at least one of us going with you?"

"Well, you are sitting in front of him," Laila said as she patted Anarani's neck. "And all I would like is to start out on my own before the rest of you leave to follow me. That way, you can make sure I am okay. Besides, I feel like my father is still very much part of the desert and would be another ally on my journey."

"But Laila, Anarani may feel like an ally, as bonded as the two of you are. But he is still a camel and you have to know your way for him to take you to the village."

"Do you not know how many caravans I have taken to that village?" Anarani commented.

Go'at's eyes grew large and he leapt up from where he sat. He stared at Anarani, then Laila. And back and forth, until he looked firmly at Laila and said, "As Allah is my witness, what did I just hear?!"

"That is what I wanted to tell you. Anarani is not just a camel, he is a talking and very aware camel who knows his way and can guide me with his deeply wise camel knowledge." Laila smiled wrapping her arms around Anarani's neck.

Go'at came a bit closer looking perplexed, much like Laila did during her first encounter. Then Go'at's face shifted to an expression of inward searching. "Oh...yes, I remember when you came to me with the look of having seen a *djinn* soon after you arrived, Laila. Was that when you heard Anarani speak for the first time?" he asked.

"Yes."

"Humpf!" Anarani interjected. "Let me make something very clear, my dear Go'at. I have had this skill since I was a young camel and have kept it silent. Only when Laila came did I let her know. I do not want this to be known by any others. I am only talking to you to help Laila."

Go'at grinned from ear to ear and, before he knew it, he started laughing so hard he collapsed on the ground holding his belly. It was so infectious Laila couldn't help but laugh as well. With all the commotion around him, Anarani got up and started walking away saying, "Now you know why I do not want to be seen and heard. I believe my job is done here. I will be off." He headed toward the vegetation for an evening snack.

"Oh, Anarani!" Laila ran to catch up. "I'm sorry. You have to admit that it's very unusual to see a camel talk. Go'at and I don't mean anything bad. There, there." She tried to pat his shoulder. He looked down, gave her his nudge of love, then continued on his way—but the expression on his face belied his annoyance.

"Don't worry, I'll make sure Go'at promises on the Tuareg honor code that he will not let anyone else know. Thank you, my amazing friend!" She gave his leg a squeeze and ran back to Go'at.

As Laila and Go'at walked back to camp, they discussed the plan about leaving on her own. He was reluctant to let her do it, Anarani or not. There could be many dangers if even alone for minutes in the desert. He wasn't sure how he would reassure the rest of the men that he had not completely lost his mind letting Laila go off on her own, since he would have to leave out the part about Anarani. But Go'at and the others knew that they had to let unfold the mysteries that were out of their hands. *Inshallah.*

## THE TUAREG HONOR CODE

"My presence, embodied by all Tuareg men and women, is to live with honor, dignity, patience, heart, and courage. The first part of my essence is *ashek*: acting with honor and dignity. This quality is grown starting in childhood so that it may accumulate as one matures to achieve a position of respect in society. Every day a person lives is a measure of *ashek* by carrying great responsibility in relation to oneself, one's family, and society. As a Tuareg saying goes, 'I would rather break my leg than break my word.' One's leg can mend, the broken word cannot. Lose *ashek* and a person is never to be trusted again.

Then there is *tasaidert*, courage and patience. This is the foundation for living in the harshness of the desert where one must walk for miles with scarcity of food and water. A Tuareg demonstrates *tasaidert*, for example, when he looks for his camels all day with nothing to drink and upon encountering a camp, engages in conversation before asking for water. And even better, he waits until the drink of water is offered.

And the final quality of my presence is *ull*, heart and will. It is the engine of the world for without heart, one has nothing. A person knows things with the heart, not with the head. If the heart doesn't beat anymore, the body is dead—one is not truly alive without heart. Getting off track from *ull* means there is a wave of heat that rushes from one's head.

Yes, I am the 'police' of the desert, the way, the path. Live by me and one always finds refuge. Without me, a person is under embargo—losing community, and thereby, life."

## LAILA'S JOURNAL ENTRY

The desert sky is like no other. At night the depth of darkness resembles a black hole, save the brilliant wash of stars as thick as the endless grains of sand below. When I slip into my sleeping bag, I diligently watch for the first pinpoint signs of starlight. It feels as if I am a child again playing a game of peek-a-boo. One blink of my eyes and a star appears. Bit by bit, as the fading dusk becomes enveloped by the night, the stars are brightly birthed, granted their essential need for darkness. For though we think the stars "disappear," they are always there above us. They just require a darkened stage on which to perform their illuminated show.

I love witnessing the crepuscular transition of night and day coexisting, holding hands side by side for precious moments. I imagine night and day embracing like lovers saying goodbye, but instead of parting ways they meld to become their beloved opposite: light to dark—and at dawn, dark to light. The quality of each is entwined within the other, even when one is more prominent. And when night comes, it brings a poetic dream-filled pause that wraps its threads around my awareness, disengaging me from the collective conscious of the day, until I awake again.

## A SAFE HAVEN IN THE VASTNESS

The next day, Go'at and Laila made preparations for her trip. This, of course, had to take place where no one at the oasis would see them since it also included Anarani. To avoid anyone overhearing their conversations, Go'at told the men that he would be taking Laila out on a practice ride with Anarani to work on safety issues and how to read cues from the sun and landscape. During his exchanges with Anarani, there were moments when Go'at could not contain his amusement at conversing with a camel. Anarani, being sensitive to these reactions, took offense and, on several occasions, turned in a huff to walk away. Laila had to intervene to assuage his irritation.

Given that they had planned to leave the oasis that day, the men were not terribly upset about the chance to relax an extra day. They also trusted Go'at's judgment about letting a young, inexperienced Westerner take off on her own. It was only five miles, and in camel power, that translated to a day. Besides, they had all decided that they would begin following Laila only an hour after she left. This would put their minds at ease while allowing Laila the independence she strongly desired to demonstrate.

The morning of Laila's departure began with the usual activities. But instead of a caravan, a lone figure on a camel left the camp. Laila trekked into the desert of her longing, uncertain of what she would find. She felt a deep desert thirst to dive into the well of emptiness she carried within. She knew that if she were to continue living within the familiar boundaries of her life, the chance of finding a sense of belonging would continue to slip away. Of the many voices she heard beckoning her to take this journey, this morning, she heard the one that had begged her to shed the modern techno-urban, possessions-filled, linear thinking world: a world of boundaries, a world steeped in fears and stress. She was glad she had followed its message. For as the seams of these boundaries loosened with each day and each experience, the emptiness she felt was being filled with the energies of nature and the wisdom of the nomads. She was also learning to trust herself, feeling an inner safe haven as she trekked the outer vastness of the desert.

## LAILA'S JOURNAL ENTRY

The morning of my trek into the desert—just Anarani and me. These past weeks, wandering as an unfettered nomad has made me focus on just being. Each day has been about my footsteps in the sand, one in front of the next. A sense of belonging is growing within. As I think about this, it occurs to me that I no longer feel as though I am sinking into the immense void of my heart. Something is shifting. I now feel a sense of safety and protection walking through the vastness of the Sahara along with the nomads and Anarani. The words that are coming up are: I am sinking into the safe haven of my heart.

Yet that tingling sensation is rising up in my gut again. It's similar to the sensation I had before leaving the comfort of my world for the Sahara. I am entering another threshold, another dive into an unknown that's already embedded in the unknown. I took a deep breath and asked—what do I really feel? A tinge of fear, yes; but that's to be expected as I venture off on my own. (And isn't there a fine line between fear and excitement?) Then I took another deep breath that allowed me to come back to the safe haven of my heart. As expansive as a void may feel, a safe haven is even more expansive. It provides me the strength to face my fears, both internal and external. I no longer shrink in the emptiness; instead I fill its vastness. Walking in the desert is like being released from a cage.

And on a more mundane note, my gut is acting up. It's reacting to the food and water, not to mention all the emotional experiences this quest has been delivering. I am sprinting quickly these days to find cover with my loosening bowels. No escaping the profane in the midst of the sacred. And so I go... in more ways than one.

## AMADOU AND HAMIDOU

Without the company of the men to interact with, the progress of their walking plodded on slowly. The sun in the afternoon sky never seemed to move; it hung like a pendulum at rest. Sitting atop Anarani, Laila appreciated the gentle rocking rhythm of his sway, much like a ship on the ocean.

"Anarani?"

"Hunh?" his ears went back to listen.

"Have you heard the saying, 'Camels are the ships of the desert'?"

"What is a ship?"

"Ha...of course. You have never been near the ocean, have you?"

"Tell me more."

"Well, if you replaced all the sand as far as the eye can see with water equally as deep, that's what an ocean looks like."

"Then walking would be very hard," he mused. "So what does a camel have to do with that much water and the word you used?"

"Instead of walking, people use ships that float through the water. The ships have space to store goods and people as they go from one place to the next. Camels and caravans perform similarly to ships, only in the dry desert conditions."

Anarani stopped, cocked his head and asked, "And what do you feed these 'ships'?"

"Oh, no, no, they're not alive! They are built by people out of wood or other materials that float." Laila laughed and gave Anarani a hearty pat on his neck.

"Anarani?"

"Hmmmm?"

"Are we walking the same path my father and mother would take to the village?"

"Yes, the same as any path can be with no roads to follow."

The day gently rolled past one long legged step to another. Laila, rocking from the motions of those long strides, felt completely connected to each moment that passed. She gave up many days ago trying to keep track of time. An osmosis-like exchange had replaced her thought-filled mind with more and more space. Then something caught her eye: a bird landed atop a hill to one side. It was a large bird. Laila was amazed. She couldn't believe her eyes.

"Anarani, look. I think it's a crane!" He stopped. "Yes, it is a crane," she confirmed. "In the middle of the Sahara, a crane!" She slid off Anarani to take in this sight.

"I have seen them and many others around this time," Anarani commented.

"They are migrating. I remember my father telling me about that. But to happen to be here at this moment! What a gift." The crane took off flapping its lanky, yet graceful wings. They watched him as he inched into a smaller and smaller spot on the expansive horizon. She climbed back up on to Anarani and they continued on, but this was a moment Laila would never forget.

As Laila gazed upon the desert landscape, a Tuareg saying she had heard from Go'at bubbled up: "Allah has taken all that is superfluous from the desert." In such a beguiling, naked environment of endless sand littered with scattered scrubby plants and rocky features, the starkness laid bare her vulnerabilities. Anarani may be her ally, but without human companionship, she knew how vulnerable she was at this moment. Venturing out into the most solitary, wild place on the planet, was unearthing a realization. By bravely stepping into her vulnerability, it was allowing her to also access the inner strength that resides in her soul and psyche. She was letting go of the protective layers around her heart the deeper she penetrated into the desert, layers that had kept her from truly feeling connected. As the vision with Aschenked taught her, it is through vulnerability that our hearts can vibrate together in greater harmony. But vulnerability paired with strength felt counterintuitive. She had to learn to trust this new lesson and the only way to do that would be putting it into practice.

Then, on the shimmering horizon, they saw ghostly forms. Anarani and Laila could not distinguish how many at first, but slowly there appeared two men riding camels, with a pack camel in tow. Anarani sniffed the air. A scent was just beginning to waft up his nose, still faint, but strong enough for him to realize the potential trouble these two held.

"Laila," he turned his head to speak as he stopped in his tracks. She threw her leg over and slid out of the saddle.

"Anarani, do you know who is approaching?" she asked.

"I don't know who exactly, but their nature, yes," he responded with a concerned tone.

"And what does that mean?"

Scents played a big part of a camel's keen observations. Humans, like any animals that live together in close proximity, share a group scent. If a family is related, an even stronger blending occurs among the members. In the Tuareg culture, there are certain classes of people who tend to group together. With the wind in his favor, Anarani sniffed two different classes of odors drifting his way.

"These are two who as individuals can drum up the *djinni* of the desert, but put them together..." he trailed off shaking his head and staring off in their direction. He then looked at Laila, "I'm telling you, you must be very quick to deal with their ways. The *djinni* are never too far from the breath that leaves their mouths."

"But Anarani," Laila chuckled, "*djinni* are from stories and fairytales. Surely you don't..."

Anarani cut her off with a gruff huff. "Laila, do not question what I have seen! Have you forgotten my story and who you are talking with right now?"

"Oh, Anarani, I-I'm sorry..."

"No time for being sorry! Quick, before they get any closer and can see me talking! I must fill you in so you can perform to counter their mischief."

With great authority he told her that these two came from the camps of the blacksmiths and marabouts. Her father had lived in those camps to study them, so Anarani was familiar with not only their smells but also their practices. Both possess mystical powers that can have contrary effects on each other. If these powers are not contained, disorder can arise as they endlessly play a tug of war between cause and remedy.

He told her about the blacksmiths' powers that are associated with the fire *djinni*. Their nature is clown-like, but they wield power by holding secrets. This makes people fear them. They embody and control *djinni*. Smiths can be seen as destructive, especially if one refuses a smith's request for a gift. Marabouts' powers are associated with water. They are the scholars of Islam. When they become priests, they are able to diagnose spirit possessions in people. Once diagnosed, the possessed are then referred to a blacksmith for exorcism of the spirit. Laila was trying to take this all in. Meanwhile the figures were inching closer and closer.

"Anarani, tell me, what do you suggest when they try to engage with us?" she asked with uncertainty.

"Us?" he said with a sardonic tone and one brow scowling.

"Alright, alright. I mean 'me', but you better help me with cues as best you can. Talk about dealing with a *djinn*!" Laila poked his neck. "Come on, let's stop wasting time. They are almost here."

"Welllll, do not smile too much, but do not be too serious. Do not talk a lot, but do not seem distant. Do not ignore the request of a gift, but do not give anything away too willingly," he advised, as he brought his face closer and closer to Laila.

"Anarani, that all sounds so contrary."

"That is exactly right!" He threw his head up.

"But how do I use this information? What do I say? I'm not sure you are helping me here," Laila said. Her eyes rolled up while her lips pursed to one side.

"You have two traits in your favor: intelligence and that you are a woman."

"What do you mean by that?" she asked with a hint of irritation, not sure if he was being facetious or not.

"They see women as less affected by the evil eye of the *djinn* than men, especially those who can have children. Women are closer to the *djinn* spirits' world. Besides," he pointed out, "you are a foreign woman and more familiar with their culture than they might think. Use that to your advantage. And speaking of advantage, get back up in the saddle. You must not be lower than them or they will have the advantage." Anarani lowered his neck so Laila's foot could take hold and be hoisted up. He started walking.

Laila could feel her heart beating. Spirits, exorcism, contrariness. It all seemed so make-believe. She told herself to take a deep breath. What was she doing in the middle of this desert ocean? Suddenly an image flashed of sailing the Sahara sand waves, Anarani her first mate by her side. She spied the pirates' flag from a distant ship coming into focus through her telescope. How was she going to navigate this one? "Dad would have known what to do," she thought. She hoped the Tamasheq she had learned would flow now.

"Dad," she whispered, "oh, let me think like you." Aschenked's question from her vision also came to her, "Are you willing to listen with the ears of your heart?" To deeply listen meant opening up to her vulnerability, and in so doing it would also feed her strength to be present and alert. At that moment, the breeze picked up. The sound of the wind rushed around her and for a second she swore she heard a voice, a word, blowing through her *shesh* into her ear.

"Am-u-let." Each syllable softly lingered to the next, allowing her to make out the word "amulet." Her amulet, the one her father gave her the last year they were here as a family. She cherished it and made sure she kept it close to her during this journey. She wore it around her neck, underneath her *gandora*. Laila reached for it under the *shesh* feeling for the yarn of the necklace to pull it out.

To anyone else it would have no aesthetic or monetary value. It was merely a small, white, cloth pouch on a strand of black yarn. On the outside of it, her name was written in very small letters in Tamasheq, and underneath that there was an Arabic symbol. Her father told her that neatly sewn within the pouch was a folded piece of paper holding a Koranic blessing. One of the marabout elders who lived in the village he had studied made it especially for Laila as a gift to her father. It was supposed to be imbued with protective powers, which she didn't quite believe, but at this moment and situation she was willing to suspend her disbelief.

Anarani turned his head as he remembered another piece of advice. "Expect the ritual greeting from these two. Be advised to follow it and don't ask them their names until they have asked yours." The ritual greeting was an ages-old formality not adhered to very readily these days, but it still lingered among the older tribal members. Laila learned of this exchange from her parents' anthropological studies. That was the last of the wisdom Anarani could offer.

Laila wasn't sure whether she should leave the amulet in sight or tuck it back under her *gandora*. She decided to wear it in full view. Why else did a voice in the wind bring it to her attention?

The camels and their riders slowly narrowed their distance and finally came to a halt. The two Tuareg trotted their camels in opposite directions around Laila and Anarani, then positioned themselves in front. Although her *shesh* was wrapped so that only her eyes showed, she knew they could tell she was a foreigner. But she wasn't quite sure if they could tell that she was a "she" yet. An awkward pause floated in the air. Laila nodded her head toward them and they returned the same. She then summoned her courage to begin the ritualized greeting.

"You are well?" she asked.

"We are well," one replied.

"On you no evil?"

"No evil," the other replied.

"Praise be to God," Laila offered.

"Praise be to God," they offered back in unison.

"How are you?"

"No evil, thank God."

"You and yours be safe?"

"We are well."

"Praise be to God."

"Praise be to God."

Laila paused hoping this covered enough of the exchange. She looked at one and the other. The creases around their eyes were as deep as parched cracks. One of them had large, round, wire-rimmed glasses giving him a scholarly look. They stared intensely back at Laila, until the spectacled one spoke.

"Ahh, and who graces us with such knowledge of our ways yet does not come from this land?"

"My name is Laila," she responded accordingly. "And who graces me with wisdom as vast as a desert horizon?" The Tamasheq flowed from her lips so far. She was amazed at the words she was summoning, but she had wisely practiced with Go'at over the course of the days they were traveling in the caravan.

"I am Amadou," said the one with the glasses.

"I am Hamidou," said the other.

Uncertain of her next words, Laila took Anarani's advice and sat with the silence, adjusting herself in the saddle to sit a little straighter and higher.

"Amadou," Hamidou spoke up looking directly at Laila, "in the name of Allah, what manner of woman is before us who wears a man's clothes, speaks our language and greeting, and is a lone traveler on this sand that matches the color of her skin?"

"Yes, Hamidou," pondered Amadou, "I do not recall an encounter such as this in all the days and nights I have journeyed these ergs and massifs, as Allah is my witness."

Laila was becoming a bit perturbed at their indirect, third-person questions about her. Her Westernized feminine hackles were starting to rise, but she checked that sensation. She wanted to maintain anthropological objectivity. Any judgment would diminish her sharpness to interact.

"And how does a sand-skinned, sky-eyed woman come by an amulet such as she is wearing?" Amadou still questioned indirectly.

"Could this be a *djinn* sent to test us?" Hamidou puzzled, leaning his head slightly sideways toward his companion while his eyes stayed fixed on Laila.

"Tell us, fair one," Amadou now directed his question to Laila, "why do you wander this land where one can never be certain of man, beast, wind, and water?"

"I walked this land many years ago in the time before the revolution," she informed them.

"Your years were young then," Hamidou surmised.

"I was here with my mother and father..." but before she could say anymore, Amadou chimed in.

"Jack and Katherine," he added without skipping a beat.

"Yes!" Laila exclaimed. Her eyes widened at hearing her parents' names. "How do you know that?"

"Your father stayed in my village. And that *gris gris* (amulet) you are wearing, it is the one I made for you," said Amadou.

Being the wise men that they were, Amadou and Hamidou knew that this was more than a chance encounter. They had just left their village to make their way into the desert. With all the tracks and routes one can traverse in all of the Sahara, they reached this particular point in time and place where their path crossed with not only a lone foreign woman, but one with a strong connection to their past. The desert *djinn* were showing their powers in a most interesting way.

"Do you know the direction that you are taking?" Hamidou asked of Laila.

"I believe the way is to the village where my father was killed," Laila replied. "My guide, Go'at, pointed me in this direction and told me it was about eight kilometers to the village."

"Yes, we just left our village on the way to another," commented Amadou. Then with a start and a furl of his eyebrow over the rim of his glasses, he looked at Hamidou saying, "Are you thinking the same thing as I?"

"We return to our village with this unusual presentation placed in our path," he echoed very closely the same thoughts as Amadou.

Laila felt another flush of independence rise up within her. She was navigating quite well on her own, not to mention having Anarani's keen sense of direction. She knew arriving alone at the village as a white woman in men's clothing would be a very strange phenomenon. However, she knew the importance of paying attention to the cues being presented now. This was no time to exert her Western independent streak. Besides, here were the elders of the village with whom she needed to connect.

"Come," Amadou smiled warmly to Laila as he turned his camel toward the direction from which he had approached. Hamidou followed suit. Laila tugged on Anarani's lead to see if he would look at her. His head swayed around as he shook it and even with one side of his head in view, she knew that he was winking his eye to provide assurance.

## LAILA'S JOURNAL ENTRY

What a strange unfolding of occurrences, but the desert is where time and space warp, outwardly as well as inwardly. One's sense of what is evaporates with the heat. The wide, frank, openness of the surroundings permeates my mind, heart, and soul. Like a distant mirage alluring me with shimmering possibilities, there is no telling what is in store. While this is true anywhere, the Sahara places me at the threshold of this awareness with every step

I take.

## A WELCOME ARRIVAL

Laila, Amadou, and Hamidou arrived at the village made up of the blacksmith and marabout families. On the way, Amadou and Hamidou let Laila know that they were heading to another village to perform an exorcism on a woman.

As Amadou said, "We must place trust in Allah that the timing of our meeting is written and therefore delaying the exorcism is part of the divine plan."

"*Inshallah*," Hamidou completed the sentiment.

The three rode most of the way in silence. Laila's mind and heart raced with questions about what was to come in relation to all that had been revealed thus far. But for this moment, she was dealing with a more pressing physical issue that she could not ignore—her gut was beginning to rumble. She was starting to feel completely out of synch with her body.

The village was an encampment where there were no permanent structures, only tents. The tents varied in structure and size. Some were round with enclosed sides, some were rectangular like a lean-to, and others were an amorphous mixture of both. The tops of the tents were covered with woven mats or red-dyed, goat-hide tarps sewn together. The hides were stretched out with poles, and the walls were made of more woven mats. The tents were clustered into two slightly separate sections to distinguish each family grouping. On one side, the tents of the marabout family were arranged in an orderly pattern—a sort of semicircular zigzag, while the smith's side looked random and scattered. Thus, it was the representation of their contradictory natures.

The timing of their arrival—just as the sun reached a languid position hovering above the horizon—provided Laila with enough light to get her bearings. A golden hue cast a warm glow on the riding party. The children ran out to greet them first, pointing and chattering excitedly about the new guest, the looks of which they did not see very often in this remote area. With this unusual arrival, the day's routine was disrupted. The children, and then the adults, began leaving their tents and chores to view the curiosity. The ruckus disturbed the resting goat herd, causing them to stand up in response and bleat their surprise in mixed tones and rhythms.

The crowd of onlookers gathered on top of each other, but at a respectable distance from Laila. Hamidou glanced at one of the young men. With that cue he came over, couched Anarani, and helped Laila off. Amadou and Hamidou dismounted their camels and came together waving their hands for their families to gather 'round. With Laila standing next to them, they spoke.

"*Bishmillah* (in the name of God)," Amadou began. "Today we have been blessed with the arrival of one who was last here as a child with her parents Katherine and Jack. He turned to Laila. "We," he motioned to Hamidou and himself, "and our families welcome you to our village once again." His hand swept through the air in an arc, indicating everyone gathered. "Laila, while you are here, we share with you all that we have, for as we say, 'If I have water and you come to me, I give you half.'"

Amadou was speaking in the Tamasheq language for his people. Laila, in the midst of her body's condition, was not at her best to concentrate and picked up only bits and pieces. She hoped her gut would stay calm not only for this introduction, but for the rest of the evening so she could concentrate on her Tamasheq skills. Luckily, with the years that her parents had studied in their village, there were English speakers with whom she could communicate, not to mention that Go'at and the other men would also be arriving.

Hamidou continued. "And so it is written that you have returned to be with our families. A daughter loved and long lost, *Inshallah*, has been found." Amadou then Hamidou gave Laila a hug as the crowd clapped, cheered, and the women ululated. Amadou walked over to one of the women to speak to her. She nodded her head and he went back to Laila.

"Come with me, Laila. You will have a place to stay." He indicated for her to follow him. He led her to a tent she could share with the woman he had just spoken to. Her name was Ami and her husband was away on caravan.

Ami readily invited Laila into her tent, which was circular and enclosed. She showed her to an area where she could lay her pad and sleeping bag. One of the other women came to the tent to offer Laila a cup of frothy camel's milk to refresh her from the day's journey. Laila accepted it hesitantly, given how her stomach was feeling. However, she did not want to appear rude, so she drank it. It tasted pleasant enough, creamier than cow's milk with a bit of a salty aftertaste. She hoped that it would settle, rather than upset, her stomach.

Ami asked her in Tamasheq if she was hungry and held out a basket of fresh dates. Laila could understand her quiet, slow delivery and shook her head in response. She didn't want to tempt fate by adding dates to the camel milk, but these offerings brought to mind the Tuareg saying that Amadou had just recited about sharing. Living in a land of scarcity comes with the understanding that at any time, one may be at the mercy of others for their generosity. Laila sat for a moment to gather her thoughts and reflect on the generous care she was being given. Her arrival was feeling more welcomed than she could have imagined.

Just then, they heard children running and yelling outside the tent. When she and Ami went out, the children again were rushing toward the same direction from which Laila had just arrived. In the distance, a small caravan was approaching. The sun had lowered its head just below the horizon. This was Go'at, Ibrahim, Ouhetta, and Baggee. Their sensibilities pushed them to leave twenty minutes after Laila and Anarani. Amadou and Hamidou welcomed their friends and led them to where they could set up their camp.

This was no longer an ordinary day.

✦✦✦

When the evening came, the entire village gathered to welcome their guests. Go'at and his men built a huge campfire for everyone to sit around. The women prepared a meal of millet and goat's meat. And as the night sky grew darker, the stars sparkling like glitter overhead, their festivities continued with drumming and dancing. Of course, Ibrahim and all the tea makers from the village worked together to brew the shai tea so everyone could imbibe the three rounds—bitter like life, strong like love, and sweet like death. Yes, Laila thought when she settled into her sleeping bag in the wee hours of the morning, what a welcome arrival.

## A MEETING OF BELLIES

Upon awakening the next morning, Laila felt lucky that her stomach had not given her much trouble during the evening's festivities, but she could tell more grumbling was on its way. Ami had already left to start her chores. She sat up a bit groggy, then heard footsteps approaching the tent.

"Laila?" She heard her name spoken softly outside the tent. When she opened the flap, there was a beautiful young woman very full with child kneeling in front of her. She wasn't sure who she was.

"Hello?" she responded quizzically.

"You don't remember me, do you?" asked the woman.

Laila furled her brows, shaking her head from side to side.

"I used to take care of you when your parents came here to be with our family."

Laila searched her mind's memories. Then suddenly she realized that the face before her matched the image she remembered when this woman was a girl. "Oh Fatima, is that you?!"

"Yes, yes!" she exclaimed. They embraced each other.

"Oh, and look at you! When is your baby due?"

"Today, tomorrow, any day! And what luck for you to arrive now. I hope you will be staying?"

"Yes. It has been a long journey to get here and I feel so welcome. And…" her voice trailed off.

"Ahh, Laila, your face gives you away. You are not feeling well?"

"No, but it has been hard to say anything to the men who guided me here. It's…" she then held her lower belly by crossing her arms over it. "My gut has not been feeling well."

Fatima nodded her head. "Don't worry. My mother, Dassine, is a healer who works with plants that can help you. With some rest and her care, you will be feeling better and you will have your strength back by the time this little one comes into the world, *Inshallah*."

"I planned on staying, and now with this event, I am even happier that I arrived when I did."

"Yes! There will be more than just one arrival to this village that our *tende* will be celebrating!" Fatima was referring to the festivities in which the women play a drum (a "*tende*"), have a camel race, sing, and dance.

"I remember the *tende*s and Anarani racing. I was excited to see him running so fast while I cheered him on." They reminisced about their childhood—how Fatima had taught Laila desert games, sitting together in the school tent learning Tamasheq, and how Fatima once rescued Laila when she was five years old and had wandered too far in search of Anarani.

"You didn't get very far, but it had your parents, and of course the whole village, worried!" Fatima laughed.

"My mother was so upset with herself that she let me out of her sight for those few minutes. I didn't realize I was in any danger. I just wanted to pet my dear camel. I thought I saw him in the distance and I was very determined to get to him so I sneaked past everyone. But you knew me very well and were already heading my direction when my mother realized." She told Fatima about the emotions she and her mother had to go through as they adjusted to life in the U.S. without her father.

"Oh, Laila so much has happened! It is so good to see you." They hugged again and when they backed away, the air became still. A lingering quiet allowed them to really see each other. Then Fatima took Laila's hands and spoke.

"Laila, in talking about when you and your parents were here, I just thought of something that I would like to ask you. But this is not the time. I think we need to get you to the women's tent so your healing can begin. Then I will make sure my father, Amadou, prepares a blessing to go inside a *gris gris* to protect you. My mother and father are a most potent pair," she said with a smile. Spying the amulet on Laila, Fatima held it in her hand and said, "And I think it is time for you to have a more beautiful *gris gris*, so I will also talk with Hamidou about making a leather and silver pouch to hold my father's blessing."

Laila tried to smile, but just then her insides took over her attention. "Oh dear," Laila said as she again held her abdomen. "I think I must run to take cover."

"Come, I'll take you to privacy." Fatima got up, took Laila's hand to help her up and they walked very quickly. Laila had to smile at the irony of a very pregnant woman helping her run to find a place to go. This welcome was more than she could have imagined. How much it felt like arriving home.

## LAILA'S JOURNAL ENTRY

Entering into the life of the village and now being in the company of women, I felt it was time to take off my *shesh*, which is not women's attire. I did not think to order a set of women's clothing, so the *gandora* will have to suffice. Luckily, I was able to change into fresh clothing to be more presentable.

Unwrapping my *shesh* in privacy, and finally looking at myself in a hand mirror, all I could say was, "Eeek!" After weeks of not showering and shoving my hair within the yards of fabric, I had "*shesh* hair"! Although the dryness of the desert doesn't promote sweating, it was quite flat and lifeless. Brushing it the best I could, I pulled it back into a ponytail. Once I freshened up, changed my underclothing, and put on a new *gandora*, I stepped outside the tent.

Ami was sifting grain in a large, round, shallow basket. When she saw me, she pointed to my head. I heard the word, "*anazadan, anazadan,*" in the phrases she spoke. I remembered that it means "hair." She took my hand and we went back into her tent. She wanted to wash my hair. I hesitated at first, but I succumbed to both her enthusiasm and the thought of finally having clean hair. We used a small bucket of water and a ladle to wet my hair. I pulled out my travel-sized bottle of shampoo, and what a treat to scrub my flattened, *shesh* hair! Once it was washed but still wet, Ami applied some ochre. My blond hair is now a reddish hue and she made a tiny braid that starts at the crown of my head and drapes across my forehead. This is a festivity braid. The rest of my hair is pulled back in a single braid. I smiled at her attempts to beautify me, and felt grateful for her willingness to set aside her daily chores to make me feel cared for.

## A *GRIS GRIS*

Amadou sat in his tent reading his Koran and praying on this sign; the presentation of Laila was beyond coincidence. This was cause to make another *gris gris* for Laila with a passage from the Koran: a blessing for the arrival of one who had deep connections to the desert and its people.

Once Amadou felt moved to prepare the blessing, he sat just outside his tent. This part of his work required connecting with all the energies of the people and the desert. On the ground in front of him, he placed a deep metal pot a shade darker than the night sky. In the pot, he mixed together charcoal powder, crushed berries, and water. This was the black ink with which he would write his blessing. He stirred the contents with a wooden spoon—it swirled 'round and 'round like a black hole—and his gaze was drawn into the vortex. Next to him was a long, wooden board with slightly curved sides made from the bark of an acacia tree. This was the blessing board on which he would write his blessings with the ink.

"*Abba* (father)," he looked up and his daughter, Fatima, was standing there. "Of course you are already preparing the blessing," she grinned.

"Ahh, it is my little *gerboa* who moves swiftly and knows all that is happening." He grinned back. "And how is our guest doing? I hope she is feeling better now that she is under Dassine's care."

"Yes, *Anna* (mother) is working her magic on her, just as you are working your magic here. I believe she will be well enough when you are ready to deliver your blessing. I will leave you to your task and find Hamidou to ask him for a special silver and leather *gris gris*."

As she turned to leave, Amadou said without looking up, "Fatima?"

"Yes, *Abba*?" she turned around.

"Go ask Hamidou if he can make a silver and leather *gris gris* for my blessing…" he looked up at her and gave her a wink while Fatima shook her head, smiling. And just as she turned around again, there was Hamidou standing so close that she nearly bumped into him.

With a start, Fatima exclaimed, "*Bishmillah*! You two are always up to something!" Amadou and Hamidou grinned widely. Fatima shook her head and spoke with a tone of annoyance, but turned to leave so that they could not see that she, too, was smiling at their antics.

Hamidou then said, "Amadou, what are you divining about Laila's arrival? The timing of her arrival is a sign from Allah, but we must resume our travels to perform our exorcism."

"Yes, yes. We will leave tomorrow morning. Last night, I journeyed through my dreams to work with the *djinn*. Their influence will be held until we arrive, *Inshallah*. Do you have a *gris gris* in which to place my blessing for Laila? With Dassine's healing, she should be well enough that I may deliver my divination when the sun kisses the horizon, *Inshallah*."

"Yes. It will be ready to receive your blessing."

# THE SECRETS OF LIFE

 Fatima made her way to the women's tent to check on Laila. She found her lying down on a mat. Dassine's finger was poised on Laila's stomach. This was a *tinesmegelen's* (medicine woman's) way of measuring the health of her patient. Fatima walked over and sat next to Laila, giving her a caring smile and stroking her head. Laila was feeling nurtured in a way she hadn't felt for a long time. She closed her eyes as Dassine massaged her stomach. Along with the massage, Dassine pronounced the Koranic benediction "*Bishmillah*," then touched the ground twice. This was to take the disease out of both patient and healer ensuring that it would be absorbed by the ground. She then took goat fat in her hand, spat on it, and administered it as a medicine on Laila's stomach in order for her blessing power to be transmitted. Dassine covered Laila with a camel blanket and nodded to Fatima.

 Fatima was learning the herbalist trade while assisting her mother. She went over to a tarp laid out with food items and various liquids in bowls. Her mother had made an infusion of millet, goat cheese, and ground dates as part of Laila's treatment. Fatima poured the thick liquid into a cup and brought it over to Dassine who handed it to Laila. She instructed her to sip the remedy slowly. They both left the tent so Laila could rest.

 With one sip, the pungent sweetness was too much for her taste buds and stomach to handle. Even the massage, as well meaning as Dassine's intentions were, made Laila uncomfortable. Now that she was alone, she closed her eyes hoping for relief through sleep. She focused on her breath. The sounds of the village carried on outside the tent. Her thoughts went to Anarani. This had been the longest time away from him since being in the desert again and she vowed, once she felt stronger, that she would seek him out. She really missed his calming presence.

 Her mindful breathing also brought up a montage of her desert experiences: her arrival in Tamanrasset, meeting Go'at and the nomads, dear Anarani talking for the first time, the tea ceremony visions with her father and Aschenked the gazelle, riding into the desert on her own with Anarani, meeting Amadou and Hamidou, her welcome into the village. This ancient, magical land, like an elder, had taken her in and was gradually revealing the secrets of life, which were not secrets at all. They were simply to quiet her mind, let go of her fears, and in so doing allowing her to connect more deeply with her heart.

## LAILA'S JOURNAL ENTRY

Dassine has worked her magic on me. I fell into a deep sleep after she treated me with her massage and infusion; neither was easy to take in. But after she and Fatima left me, I had very strong experiences with the earth and within my dreams.

Lying there physically drained, I became aware of my heartbeat. It wasn't racing, but I felt its rhythm more than usual. I wondered what Dassine did to enhance its beat. Or maybe my energy relaxed enough to be more in tune with it pumping the lifeblood through my veins. The pulse radiated out into my extremities. When it reached my head, it began spinning. Flashes of this journey swirled up, along with a flood of emotions. Even though I was lying down, it felt as though my head was floating, so I instinctively reached my hands out and dug my fingers into the sandy floor of the tent to anchor myself. Then there came a sensation I had never felt before.

Buried in the sand, my hands began to vibrate. I wasn't sure if it was the rhythm of my heart coursing down into the sand, or if the rhythm was entering me from the earth. I took a few deep breaths to center myself and realized it felt like a rhythmical exchange. My body was sinking into a deeper connection. The rhythm of my heart was beating with the rhythm of the earth. My whole body was truly coming alive, experiencing the vibration of the living world.

In the midst of these sensations, I understood something: as much as my own heart has felt pain, fear, sadness, joy, and grief, the earth has witnessed these emotions in all beings throughout time. I no longer felt separated from animals, plants, land, sunlight, rain, and wind. They, much like the blood flowing within my body, are the rhythm of life. I became overjoyed. The vast void of the unknown within my heart no longer felt foreboding. My heartbeat has always been grounded to the earth, and thus, it is also connected to the immense and expanding heartbeat of the universe. These realizations calmed me and lulled my weary body into the sleep it was longing for.

## A JACK IN THE BELLY

"Laila, Laila." Fatima gently rocked Laila's body to wake her. She had been sleeping all day, but now she was screaming.

"Wake up."

Laila was having a hard time extracting herself from the dream that still wrapped around her awareness.

"Laila?"

"Mmmm," she couldn't form words yet, nor open her eyes.

"It's Fatima. I'm here," she said reassuringly stroking her head and humming. Fatima saw how Laila was having a hard time leaving the dream world. Finally, Laila opened her eyes squinting, although there was very little light penetrating through the tent. She looked up at Fatima.

"Ahh, welcome back," Fatima gave her a smile.

"My dream, it was so intense. I was trying to save my father." Fatima got up to fetch a ladle of water for her.

"Here, you have gone a long time without water. Drink." She handed it to Laila who downed it quickly. She didn't realize how thirsty she was until the moisture bathed her throat. Fatima gave her more. "I am here to take you to my father so you can receive his blessing. If you can remember your dream, you can share it with him. That is, if you want to. An exchange of the spirit world will be very powerful."

Fatima helped Laila sit up when she was ready.

"How long have I been asleep?"

"It was morning when my mother and I left you, and the sun is just lowering on the horizon. Are you hungry?"

"I am famished, but my stomach is still a bit unsettled."

Fatima went over to the food, herbs, and containers of liquid sitting in the tent. She dipped the ladle in a bowl that held a thick porridge and put some in a bowl, sprinkling sugar over it. "Here, this is cooked millet. Take a few bites for energy," she said as she handed Laila a spoon and the bowl. Laila was delighted at the sweet, corn-like taste. She downed the portion in an instant. Laila's eyes glowed with hungry enthusiasm, which Fatima understood as she refilled the bowl.

"I'm glad to see you are feeling better." Fatima handed her the bowl and sat down in front of Laila. The surroundings were quiet except for conversations outside the tent. Laila finished the second serving of the millet, then handed the empty bowl back while shaking her head to indicate that she did not need more. Fatima placed the bowl on the ground and took a deep breath.

"Laila, I have been thinking about the timing of your arrival. You have stepped back into our village just when my belly is full with my first child. I feel it is time that I ask you an important question and I hope it will not just bring you sadness." She paused as she took Laila's hands in hers. "I, and the other women, believe that I carry a boy. If that is so, I am asking you for the honor of giving him your father's name, 'Jack'."

Laila looked in Fatima's eyes, feeling a mixture of joy and grief as tears spilled onto her cheeks. She closed her eyes long enough to temper the emotions she felt so she could form the words, "The honor would be deeply mine. I grant you permission in the memory of my dear father." With that, they hugged, sharing tears that ran the spectrum of their feelings on this momentous occasion.

## DARKNESS INTO LIGHT

Amadou was sitting in his tent awaiting Laila. His blessing board was beside him with the pot of ink and his Koran in front. Hamidou was also there, his newly-crafted, beautiful *gris gris* laid out. The square silver piece that covered the black leather was inscribed with Laila's name in Tifinagh script. Fatima brought Laila in, gave her a hug, and left. Amadou indicated for Laila to sit in front of them.

"How are you feeling, Laila?" Amadou asked.

"A bit weak and tired, but better."

He nodded to her response and closed his eyes. When he opened them, he took a deep breath and said, "You have bravely journeyed back to a place that brought pain to your heart as a child. We who remember your father also carry that pain. Many cycles of this world have passed since you left this village. I have been praying in the name of Allah since your return to our village."

Amadou picked up his Koran. "Your will and character is strong to make this quest. I feel this blessing should contain the energy of your spirit, so I will ask you to be a part of the divination. Listen to what I tell you. When I begin to chant, close your eyes and conjure up a question, an image, a dream. Allow whatever it is to present itself and do not second-guess or discount it. Be with it. I am placing this Koran here." He placed it in front of Laila. "When you are ready, use this stylus." He handed it to her. "Feel in your heart where to place the stylus to open the Koran. Then feel the passage you are drawn to. Do not worry that it is in Arabic. When you are ready, place the stylus on the page. This will be the blessing. Do you understand what I am asking?"

Laila nodded her head.

"Do you have any questions?"

Laila shook her head.

"Then *Bishmilla*h..." and he started to chant.

Laila closed her eyes and in an instant, the dream she awoke from presented itself. She wasn't surprised to see these images replaying in her mind. Tears of sadness welled up as she saw her attempt to save her father's life. She took deeper breaths to keep her composure. Amadou's chanting also gave her comfort. When the dream subsided, she sat for a few more minutes to center her energy. Then she opened her eyes, looked down at the Koran with a gentle focus, and readied the stylus. With a deep breath, she leaned forward and put the stylus between two pages and opened up the holy book. Shutting her eyes again, she poised the instrument over the pages and came down to touch the surface.

Once Amadou had finished chanting, he bent forward and put his head on the ground in prayer. Hamidou followed suit. They did this three times, and sat up. With his hands together in front of his chest, Amadou lowered his head contemplatively placing his lips on the tips of his fingers. Next, he picked up the Koran and spoke.

"This message will not only bless you, but our whole community. You are here to deepen the connection your parents forged. And so our hearts are connected." With that, he chanted her chosen verse, then translated it: "He is the One Who sends to His Servant Manifest Signs, that He may lead you from the depths of Darkness into the Light and verily Allah is to you most kind and Merciful." (Surat al-Hadid 57:9)

This verse sparked an image from her dream—the part where she was trying to save her father. Amadou saw an expression of distress on Laila's face, for not all blessings conjure joy. He knew that it was perfectly matched, as blessings usually were, *Inshallah*.

"Laila, I see in your face the effect of hearing these words. Let me know what has come up for you."

She cleared her throat and asked Amadou to repeat the verse, which he did. "I had a dream this morning. I was with my father and it had darkness and light."

"Can you tell me your dream?" Amadou asked.

"It begins in a house with my mother and father. My father is going to the door to protect us from something, but I plead with him not to go out. I fear that he will die. As he opens the door, I grab his other hand. The strong wind almost knocks us down. I plead for him to close the door, but he keeps going. I desperately cling to his hand. We fight our way into the force of the wind and suddenly we are walking in a dark cave. In the distance there is an opening with light streaming in. Walking toward it, we see two sleeping animals on either side of the opening: a cheetah and a jaguar. I hesitate, but my father wants to go past them. He motions for me to stay, and before I know it, he runs toward the opening, waking up the cats. He distracts them so I can get out safely. They look angry and hungry as they run after him. I am trying to catch up, yelling, 'Dad! Dad!' I don't want to give up. I want to save him. Then Fatima was shaking me to wake up."

Amadou and Hamidou had their eyes closed while Laila spoke. Silence blanketed the air. Sitting in this safe space with her dream being heard so deeply, Laila felt emotional, but also calm. Simultaneously, Amadou and Hamidou opened one eye and cocked their heads to look at each other. Amadou nodded his head to Hamidou, and they both looked at Laila.

Hamidou began, "Your dream holds powerful images. It also holds deep sadness. Where there is one way of feeling or being in life, there is always another. Opposites, whether they are extreme or subtle, are the nature of life. Power can be found within sadness. Light is contained in the dark. When you reverse these statements they are still true.

"You love your father. That remains. And therefore, you will always be sad and wish to save him from the harm that befell him. You cannot reverse what happened in his life, but you can learn to walk with its impact on yours." Hamidou looked to Amadou, and he continued.

"The verse and the dream that came to you speak of going forth from darkness into light. The journey of life is not always pleasant and holds danger, but Allah in his infinite wisdom will always show those with a pure heart the way that is merciful. Your father was making the way safe for you. Although the cheetah and the jaguar may seem threatening, they come as powerful guides. Each possesses a different nature—one runs like the wind; the other moves silently through the shadows. Ally with these animals in your life. Do not fear them. So Allah has brought them to you, he will help bring you forth from darkness into light."

Amadou then took the stylus from Laila, dipped it in the ink, and began writing the verse in Arabic on the blessing board. "Laila, in our tradition, we not only write the blessing on a piece of paper to place in a *gris gris*, like this one that Hamidou made for you to wear, but we also drink it in. Are you willing to drink the words of Allah and the power of their message from this blessing board?"

"Yes," Laila responded.

Amadou set out an empty bowl and rested one end of the blessing board in it. He tipped another bowl with water over the top of it, allowing the water to cascade over the writing. The ink collected in a pool of dark violet blue. When he was finished, he put the bowl in the palm of his hand and brought the other just over the top to swirl the inky, blessed water while whispering prayers over it. His eyes were closed and when he opened them, he offered the bowl to Laila. She took it from him, brought it to her lips, and slowly imbibed a bit of the concoction. She paused, and finished it off. It wasn't a pleasant drink, but at least the bitterness was only a small quantity. Amadou handed her a cup with water so she could swallow down any residue that remained in her mouth.

He then reached into the pocket of his tunic and pulled out a piece of paper so he could write the blessing for the *gris gris*. Once he folded the paper, he handed it to Hamidou and whispered prayers as Hamidou placed it in the pouch. He then leaned forward to put it over Laila's head.

Amadou said, "Laila, you have received the words of Allah to bless your body and spirit. May this carry you safely through your journey here in the desert and when you return to your home, *Bishmillah*."

Laila looked down at her new *gris gris* next to the old one. The leather and silver was so refined next to the now-worn fabric and yarn *gris gris* from her father. She looked up saying, "*Tenemert*, Amadou. *Tenemert*, Hamidou. Your wise words and insights will keep working on me, I'm sure. I have much to contemplate."

Hamidou then spoke, "Amadou and I also feel that it is time

to share information about the tragic attack that took place here." He looked at Amadou who nodded back. Laila felt her heartbeat quicken.

Hamidou continued, "When the shooting ended, and I felt it was safe enough, I sent two young men to track in the direction of the shots. They headed for the surrounding mountains. I chose these men and their camels for their swiftness. They also knew the terrain as well as any wild animal. The mildness of the wind was on their side, as it had not erased tire tracks going toward and continuing behind the mountains. In their pursuit, they spied a camp the next evening with two men. Once these men went to sleep, they checked the tread of the tires and found it matched the impressions of those near our village. The men were gendarmes, part of the army that the revolution was up against.

"By the time they brought that information back to the village, you and your mother had already left. We tried to report this to the authorities, but little was done in an atmosphere charged with rebellious events and brutal military suppression.

"There is no way to know why they targeted our village, if they took random shots, or if they meant to shoot your father. Only Allah carries that wisdom. We thought it was right to tell you of our findings."

Laila was surprised that she took these words in with little emotional reaction, although her insides felt like they were filled with lead shot. She recalled the vision from the tea when she and her mother were next to her father's body. Right now she could relate to the little girl being hugged by her mother, not quite able to fully process what she was told. Her eyes remained fixed on a spot on the ground just beyond Amadou and Hamidou.

"Laila, we are here if you want to talk about this," Amadou broke the silence. "We knew this would be difficult, but it did not seem right to keep it from you."

With a slight shudder of her head, Laila brought her focus back to the two wise faces in front of her and said, "During my journey here, clues were presented about what you described. Learning about my father's death was part of what I was seeking in coming here. There is no way to know the absolute truth and, in some ways, I feel content with the uncertainty."

Amadou and Hamidou knowingly shook their heads. Hamidou offered, "You are welcome in our village for as long as you want to stay." Then Amadou said, "Know that it is our honor to have you." Laila bowed her head with thanks and reverence to Amadou and Hamidou and left the tent.

## THE OASIS OF YOUR SPIRIT

Laila was feeling very nostalgic for Anarani and Go'at. It had been a couple of days since she had seen them. Making her way to where the men were camped, she saw Go'at in his kitchen and kneeled next to him.

"Ahh, Laila, it is so good to see you looking better."

"Yes, I feel better than when I arrived."

"It looks like you received a new *gris gris* with your blessing," Go'at said as he observed it around Laila's neck.

"Yes, I just came from the blessing with Amadou and Hamidou."

"And..." Go'at surmised. "There is something else I see in your eyes?"

Laila looked at Go'at, took a deep breath, and said, "Oh Go'at, they also told me something about my father's death. Between their words, my visions, and something Anarani revealed, I think he may have been murdered." Go'at came over and put his arm around her shoulders. "I'm okay, strangely," she said as she smiled at him. They sat down on the ground and Laila continued, "But it was so long ago and there was so much turbulence. I don't think we will ever know for sure."

"With revolutions there are many consequences that never find justice. That is the nature of living in an oppressive government. I have known this situation with my brother. He went off to train in the military camps. My family and I will never know what happened to him. We have inquired many places over the years, but there are no records."

"I'm so sorry, Go'at." They sat in the deep sadness of their shared circumstances. For no matter where strife and struggle takes place, their harsh effect on the heart knows no boundaries.

Go'at tapped Laila's knee. When she looked up, there was that gleam in his eyes as he said, "I was going to look for you. I have something to give you." He got up and motioned her to follow him to where the camel saddles and packs were sitting. He went to a pack, pulled out a bundle wrapped in brown paper, and handed it to her.

"What is it?" she asked.

"Go on, open it up," he responded.

She stooped to untie the string around it. As she opened the paper, she saw what looked like folded dark indigo robes and a veil edged with wide, silvery, decorative stitching. Her eyes got wide. "Oh Go'at, is this a woman's robe and veil?"

"Yes! You sent more than enough money, so I bought it in case you wanted to walk as a woman, rather than as a man." He smiled with a look that was whimsical, yet deeply wise.

"Oh, I can't believe it!" She hugged the garments to her. "You really look out for me…" and the excitement in her voice toned down a bit as her arms dropped still holding the robe and veil, her eyes staring off in the distance.

"Laila?"

Her thoughts went to her father and how she had never experienced him seeing her grow up to be a woman. Here was Go'at giving her a woman's outfit and in that instant it thrust her back to those awkward years as a teenager.

"I'm remembering my father." She sighed then brought her focus back to Go'at. "I wish he were here…and yet I'm very grateful to be here now with you. Oh Go'at—this time with you, Anarani, and in the village is giving me the chance to feel my life in a different way. I'm observing it as much as I'm living it." She chuckled. "Funny. That's exactly what my parents did as anthropologists. I didn't realize how much I do the same thing. But here in the desert, the observation is magnified even more."

"It is said that, 'For the body, the desert is a place of exile, whereas for the spirit, the desert is a paradise.' If we focus always on keeping up our strength in life, our spirit suffers. Strength is good, but too much and it builds resistance and protection. The challenges of the desert wear down the body's strength and resistance, which gives our spirit a chance to finally bubble up like water in a lush oasis. You are in the oasis of your spirit now that the desert has worn you down."

"Yes, I feel that all my defenses are down and all in a good way. *Tenemert*, Go'at. Thank you for all your care and wisdom and guidance. To think of bringing these clothes…Well, I will say it— you feel like a father to me. If that is okay to say." She smiled shyly with tears in her eyes.

"Of course! You are the daughter that I never had." He gave her a hug while she wiped her eyes. Then Laila laid the clothes in the wrapper to protect them until she could change into them some other time.

And in the distance they heard a soft shoosh, shoosh, shoosh of footsteps on the sand. A lone camel was shuffling toward them. They smiled at each other, knowing it could only be Anarani. Laila gave Go'at a final hug and ran toward her favorite camel. She threw her arms around his chest. Anarani nuzzled her head. She knelt down to undo the tether around his front legs. She gave Go'at a sign that they were going away from the camp and he gave her the universal thumbs up in response.

Walking over the flat terrain that grounded the distant mountains, Laila told Anarani how much she missed him. She also spilled forth her experiences in the village with verbose enthusiasm. Her faithful companion soaked up her words while chewing his cud. When they reached an acacia tree, they sat in its shade. Laila settled up against his shoulder sharing what she had just learned about her father. Anarani nodded his head. His eyes, underneath thick lashes, took on a melancholic expression. And they did not utter another word so they could savor the comfort of each other's company.

## RHYTHM, TIMING, AND PEACE CRANES

Laila fell into the rhythm of village activities, figuratively and literally. She observed and helped out in the kitchen tent making meals. One of her favorite activities was joining the women in grinding dates. This entailed using tall wooden pestles in deep wooden mortars to pound the dates into tiny bits, or into a fine powder. Two women would grind in one mortar with a repetitive up and down rhythm of their arms. It reflected the beats Laila heard when the women clapped and played their *tende* after their chores were done.

Fatima lent a slim dress and veil to Laila that she could not use during her pregnancy. Laila was looking forward to changing out of her *gandora* now that she was more in tune with the women. As well-meaning as Go'at had been in buying the feminine clothing for Laila, the women had a good chuckle at the impracticality; what he purchased was solely worn for special occasions and celebrations. They were more formal, made from a stiffer material. "Ahh, but that is the view of our men. They want us to look beautiful. But we must be comfortable as we take care of our daily tasks," Fatima commented to Laila as she looked in her hand mirror to apply kohl around her eyes. As much as practical matters dictated life, the Tuareg also held a deep sense of personal beauty, which was part of their daily routine.

Fatima had come back to her family's village to give birth. She and her husband lived in Tamanrasset. While it was the tradition for a woman to return to the village of her family without her husband, Fatima did not do so according to this dictate. In her conversations with Laila, she talked about maintaining the identity of her culture while also becoming a modern woman. As Fatima said to Laila, "I come here because I want to share this happy occasion with my family who would not be able to leave their traditional life in the village." Her husband, who ran a store with Tuareg handicrafts, stayed behind for his business. He would have to join her later, after the baby was born.

In preparation to give birth in such a remote area, Fatima had previously asked one of the village women to join her in Tamanrasset for training in a midwife program at the hospital. It would not only benefit her, but would bring a very necessary skill to the outlying areas. Menna, the newly trained midwife, would be able to take her knowledge into other villages, since even simple complications during childbirth could have tragic outcomes in the remotest parts of the desert.

After her arrival in the village, the women had assisted Fatima with setting up her birthing tent. She honored the tradition of placing it just beyond, and to the south, of the village. This was considered the female direction. The tent was draped with a great number of brightly colored blankets. One side was open, facing away from the village and out toward the desert. The floor was also strewn with blankets and straw mats. A variety of amulets were hung from the tent poles as protection from the *djinnis* of the spirit world.

With her love of babies and children, Laila was thrilled that she stepped into the village in time for this new arrival. It gave her great amusement when the children covertly followed her as she walked around. They were both shy and fascinated by this unfamiliar sight of a blond, fair, blue-eyed person. Laila, in order to connect with them, would sit very still on the ground. Little by little, the braver ones would slowly approach. Laila drew funny pictures in the sand, enticing them to come closer out of curiosity. Eventually they gathered near and started drawing pictures next to hers.

Once she gained their trust, Laila started to teach the children a few words in English. She would speak a word in Tamasheq, then write the English translation in the sand as she did her best to crudely draw the related objects. They repeated after her in unison until they were able to say the word on their own. Once they got it, they jumped around repeating it over and over, finally tumbling on her in a happily squirming pile. She didn't mind it, but their parents rushed to protect Laila from all those flailing arms and legs.

And then Laila mesmerized them by pulling out her pack of origami paper to fold into peace cranes. When she first handed the paper to them—with the bright colors and bold patterns or with a shiny finish—they would look at and feel each sheet intently. Their usual boisterous energy became very focused as they watched Laila make each fold. Once a crane was complete, she would hand it to the child who had that paper. For those old enough, she patiently taught them how to make each fold. Each child gave Laila a wide grin and a hug as they received this tiny gift. Nomadic life does not lend itself to an abundance of material possessions, so this was a small treat that did not weigh that lifestyle down. Laila was so happy that she made a point of bringing these little gems of delight with her.

## ANOTHER WELCOME ARRIVAL

The fourth morning of her stay, Laila awoke to the sound of rushing footsteps and the voices of women shouting around the camp. Ami was quickly getting herself together to leave the tent. Laila asked her in Tamasheq what was happening. Ami responded with the word "*araow*" and Fatima's name. When the word finally registered, she shot up asking Ami, "Fatima, baby?!" Ami nodded her head as she dashed out. Laila scrambled out of her sleeping bag and pulled on her clothes. In her excitement, she forgot her sandals and had to run back into the tent to put them on. Still sleepy and with the dawn's light just crowning the horizon, she wasn't sure which direction to go. One of the women rushed by, so she followed her.

When she reached the tent, Laila stopped, not certain whether to enter. As welcome as she felt, she didn't want to rush in for such an intimate event. Women were going in and out, bringing buckets of water and towels. Laila was standing to one side when she saw Dassine coming out.

"Laila! Come! Come! Join us for this happy time!" She took Laila's hand and brought her into the tent.

Laila saw Fatima squatting, holding on to her midwife Menna. Surrounding her were five other women, including Ami. They provided support by placing their hands on her back, or by allowing Fatima to hold on to their neck or shoulders. One of the women had her young daughter with her. The women chattered while Menna coached Fatima as she pushed, shifted, and occasionally uttered sentences or groans. Laila heard that Fatima had been in labor throughout the night, and this morning the women had come in anticipation of the birth.

Menna instructed Fatima and the women on positioning. Fatima was pushing through the labor as well as her exhaustion, asking if the baby would ever come. She wrapped one arm around the midwife and the other around one of the women, lowered her head, and summoned strength she didn't think she had. The rest of the women took her cue and huddled closer. Laila saw Fatima's head come up as her body forced the final push.

The midwife caressed the baby as it emerged and removed the mucous from its mouth. As it began to cry, the midwife announced, "It is a healthy boy. We thank Allah." Fatima lay down while the midwife tied a string around the umbilical cord to cut it. She wiped the blood off of the baby and asked for more towels to clean Fatima. She then laid the baby on top of Fatima. She beamed as her eyes drank in his beauty and vulnerability. Dassine stroked her daughter's head. Fatima slowly began to take in her surroundings and saw Laila off to the side. She reached out her hand and Laila came over to take it.

"Thank you for being here. It will bring good luck for Jack." She smiled at Laila.

Laila smiled back with tears streaming down her face and said to her, "I am so happy for you! He is beautiful!"

The midwife instructed, "Dassine, take the baby. Fatima, you are not done. The placenta."

The women helped Fatima get up. Minutes passed while she pushed again. When the placenta came out, Laila saw the women pile sand over it. Menna pointed in the direction of the mountains and instructed them to bury the placenta. One of the women took charge of this task. She wrapped the placenta in a towel. Next, she put incense in a bowl, lit it, and fanned the smoke all around Fatima, who was resting on the ground; the woman then placed the bowl next to her. Dassine told Laila that it was a tradition to use incense to protect a mother from malevolent or jealous *djinnis*, since the baby is still connected to the spirit world. The woman then picked up the towel with the placenta and waved the incense around it. She carried it out of the tent to bury it, walking quite a distance until Laila could barely see her.

The baby was also wrapped up, and various women attended to him so Fatima could recover. Laila was impressed that Menna was using surgical gloves and was told about her midwife training. When Dassine took the baby in her arms, Laila came over to take a closer look. She was amazed at his round face, full head of hair, and robust size. He was very healthy, indeed. Dassine held him out to Laila. She looked at Dassine with a bit of trepidation, but she gave her a reassuring nod, so Laila took the bundle. She loved holding babies, but this was her first newborn.

"Hello, Jack," she whispered. This was the first time he heard his name. She felt the newness in her arms and a strange sense of the portal that had delivered him. The series of events that brought her here at this particular moment was exquisite. And in the wake of learning about the tragic history of her own life, here was a new life unaware of all that and yet carrying on the name of a person whose stories would be told. What a welcome arrival for Fatima, the village, Laila, and the honor of her father. As she gazed into this fresh, new face, Laila felt how the time and space that held her father's death and this birth were entwining together.

## LAILA'S JOURNAL ENTRY

How does one live the edge between life and death? Today I felt such joy holding a newborn baby in my arms. There is nothing more hopeful than gazing into innocent eyes that hold every possibility for the future. And as I spoke his name, "Jack," my father's name, the well of grief surged like never before. I began to cry. I tried to hold it in on this joyous occasion, but the geyser was out of my control. Dassine, so gifted with intuition, held out her arms to take Jack and looked into my eyes reassuringly. She nodded with understanding as she moved her gaze to the opening of the tent and nodded again, indicating I should be with my lament.

Leaving the closeness of the tent to step into the expanse of the open desert, I was able to take deep breaths. I closed my eyes and turned to face the warm, dry breeze that wicked the tears from my cheeks. Stilling my mind, I felt joy and grief, both equally intense, mingling inside of me.

My heart sang with joy for the connections I now have with the village, especially through the birth of Jack. And yet as I walked, it was on the sand of deep grief where my father was ripped from my life. Joy in my heart while walking a path of grief. Is there any resolve: one or the other? Do these have to be mutually exclusive? All these years I tried to be safe by avoiding either joy or sorrow. Finally, I heard my dark heart. I had kept it in the shadows so long, but I couldn't ignore its message. The message was: Live your life, even the shadows. Live your life on the edge between darkness and light, life and death—it's about embracing the edge of discomfort, not about looking for resolve.

## EMBRACING TRADITIONS

As Fatima's strength returned, so too deepened her bond with baby Jack. Laila went with the women of the village to see Fatima and the baby over the next several days. The women would circulate in and out helping to keep Fatima nourished, and to clean out any soiled towels and linens. Laila helped Dassine with her healing remedies, and held Jack. Because she was not a mother herself, some of the women were a bit reticent to have Laila caring for Jack. But Fatima and Dassine granted her this task, observing how intuitive she was with children and how easily she cradled Jack. For the most part, he was not a fussy baby. With all the hair on his head and such refined features, he had a mature and wise look. Laila spoke Jack's name softly while he stretched and made dainty infant grunting noises in her arms. She loved to rock him until he fell asleep.

That whole week after Jack was born, preparations were

taking place in the village for the *tende*—the celebration and official naming day after a baby's birth. Before Amadou and Hamidou left to perform the exorcism, they had been charged with picking up couscous in the oasis village to be brought back for the celebration. They also returned with produce: tomatoes, beets, carrots, onions, dates.

Two days before the *tende*, the women gathered together to begin cooking the feast. With a larger volume of food to serve, three cooking areas were set up. Each one had three concrete blocks arranged to form a space in which to make a fire. Large pots were set on top. The energy around the kitchen tent increased as everyone took on a task. Some peeled vegetables, some pounded dates, and others made a special drink, *eghajira*, which consisted of pounded millet, dates, and cheese mixed with water. The ingredients were carefully poured into a goatskin, which still had the fur on the outside of it. It was then hung horizontally so the women could easily agitate the contents.

Once the vegetables were prepared, there were women who began making a stew with them in the huge pots. Laila enjoyed helping out with whatever task needed doing. The women deeply shared a particular rhythm of life. They lived very connected with one another and with their tasks. This bond extended to the way in which they beautified themselves with make-up and henna painted on their hands. The *tende* preparation and event deepened their sisterhood even more.

❁✣❁

Fatima was beginning to feel like herself again. It was a quiet time of the day. Dassine finished massaging Fatima's lower back and propped her up to make her comfortable. Laila brought Jack over. As soon as Fatima pulled him close, he turned his head and began to suckle.

"So, Laila," Fatima said as she placed folded material under Jack to support him while he breastfed, "I hear you have also been helping in the kitchen preparing for the naming ceremony. Did you think you would be put to work when you came here? Caring for a baby and cooking?" She smiled.

"Are you kidding? I'm so glad I'm not in the way and can contribute! I really appreciate how everyone helps me feel like I am part of the community."

"That is the way of our land and people. We welcome those who come because distances between desert encampments are so vast. In the desert, nothing is taken for granted, and community is almost as important as water," Dassine explained.

On the evening before the naming day, the older women came to the birthing tent for their tradition of offering the baby a secret name. Although in this circumstance, it was already known; the baby would informally be called Jack. The ritual began with women chanting and circling the tent three times in a procession while carrying Jack. The first woman in the procession was from the blacksmith community and whetted two knives together, while the second woman in line carried Jack. The ceremony would be completed the next day by using the knives to shave his hair. After the procession, the women brought Fatima her evening meal. She had spent the week recovering in the birthing tent, but in the morning Fatima would be going back to her own tent.

It was traditional for one of the blacksmith women to gather up all of the blankets and mats and take them out of the camp to bury in the sand. The next morning, the blacksmith woman charged with this task and the baby's haircutting returned to the birthing tent, along with those who had attended Fatima's labor. The blacksmith woman carried a tray with millet, dates, cheese, and incense along with a comb and the knife from last night's ritual. Shaving the infant's hair was a symbol of severing his ties with the spirit world. They wet the baby's hair, rotated the tray counterclockwise three or four times above his and Fatima's heads. And then they shaved off all of his newborn hair. Laila was secretly sad to see Jack's thick, beautiful locks shaved off. He must have felt the same way too because he wailed the moment the knife touched his head. The woman from the blacksmiths patiently and slowly shaved his hair as Fatima cradled baby Jack.

Fatima told Laila that her father was keeping the tradition of the maternal grandfather choosing an Islamic name to suit the child.

"Do you know what he chose?" Laila asked.

"Yes. It will be Sabur which means 'patient'." She laughed as Jack squirmed and fussed in her arms. "Of course, he is not exactly behaving in accordance with this meaning at the moment. Though Sabur will be his formal name, 'Jack' is what the family and women will use the most."

"Sabur Jack," Laila tried out the combination. "I'm sure that will be a very unusual name. I wish for it to bring him unusually good things in his life." She reached out for his tiny hand. He was beginning to calm down. It seemed he had finally resigned himself to the shaving.

## THE *TENDE*

"I am both the drum and the celebration. The tautness of my skin vibrates from hands playing ancient rhythms passed down from generation to generation, from mother to daughter. When I am played, I call out to the people to gather, my buoyant beat accompanied by lilting songs. They gather to celebrate life and any occasion in which joy heightens the rhythm of their hearts. Where there is rhythm, there is life. And every facet of life contains rhythm, from the smallest of particles to the deepest reaches of space. Don't be fooled that the world is silent, for there are ever-present rhythms. The insects that chirp, the birds that sing, the seasons that pass, the water that flows, the pulse of your blood. I celebrate them all, ecstatically."

## LAILA'S JOURNAL ENTRY

When it was time to dress for the *tende*, Ami and I went to her tent. She helped me don the formal dress and veil from Go'at by wrapping the material around my body. It seems like it was just yesterday that Go'at was wrapping the *shesh* around my head. I can't help but note the metaphorical significance. As I began this journey, I felt a deep restlessness and was scared about the unknowns. My head was wrapped up in battling chatter. But as I made my way here, I faced those voices in my head. There was less to fear than my mind was telling me. Unwrapping the stories, not buying into the veneer of protection, I am sinking into the depth of my heart and soul. I live not just in my mind, but am able to inhabit my body with joy.

And so yesterday I washed my body in a simple bucket of water. It wasn't the shower I craved, but it was refreshing. Today as the dark indigo material came in contact with my skin, I became tinted. There was no getting away from the effects. My hands and face became smudged. I have to say that on white skin it looked more like a dirty film that needed washing off. On darker skin the hue is richer and bluer.

There was a moment, as Ami stood in front of me to place the veil over my head, when our eyes met. It was a sisterly exchange, or at least the way I imagine it would be to look at a sister. We were initially shy about it, but our faces broke out into big smiles, expressive and heartfelt, and then we just giggled. We couldn't stop laughing. It was a connection that spoke not so much in knowing each other for years, but to the richness that comes with immersing one's heart in another culture and therefore getting to know the people who are part of it. If my father had not died, I may have had a chance to return to this community over the years; but that is not for me to lament. What matters is that I am here now because I followed my restless longing to return to this magical place and its people.

This thought brings up my vision with Aschenked, the gazelle, and the vibrations I felt through the earth. Everything, all beings, vibrate with energy. And each entity has its own pattern of vibrations. That's a lot of vibrating! And those vibrations are continually shifting and changing, much like the sand and dunes that are constantly in motion from the oscillations of the wind. Sometimes there is peace and harmony, and other times dissonance. I am grateful I stopped, listened, and followed a path deep into the dissonance within myself. It compelled me to come here, to explore and discover the nature of my vibrations and rhythms. By taking this time, my ability to stay grounded has grown, regardless of what outer vibrations I encounter. For as a desert proverb says, "The more you stop, the farther you go."

## THE *TENDE* BEGINS

Later in the day, the women gathered and the *tende* began. It was held in an area just beyond the village. They were dressed in their finest clothing, with kohl around their eyes, lips stained with a red dye, and henna painted on their hands. The drum was the center of their attention. Two of the women sat down on either side of a wooden frame that held the drum. Their hands beat the rhythm while they sang a simple, cyclical song. The rest of the women surrounded them clapping and singing. Ami had taken time to teach Laila the words of the songs, so she heartily joined in. Periodically, women ululated, as did Laila.

Fatima looked quite beautiful in a deep, rich maroon colored dress and matching veil covered with evenly patterned gold shield shapes. Her veil was wrapped high as a headdress. Dangling from her ears were large silver hoop earrings. Around her neck was a *chatchat* necklace, which had numerous small, triangular, silver pendants with black beads strung in between. Because of her husband's job as a shopkeeper in Tamanrasset, Fatima had access to a variety of goods. Through their generosity over the years, the men and women of the village had been recipients of many gifts and adornments. So the colors and patterns of their formalwear varied, especially on the young women who were eager to try new things. The older women kept with the traditional indigo style. Baby Jack was swaddled in a colorful green and yellow patterned wrap topped with a T-shirt. Fatima sat on the periphery of the singing circle, busy tending to her newborn's needs and breastfeeding him. As he grew fussy, she would get up to gently sway back and forth with Jack.

The women's singing summoned the men, also dressed in their finest. Their *gandoras* and *sheshes* were made of shiny, crisp material and smoothly wrapped much higher than usual. Some joined by riding on their camels, whose long legs pranced proudly, their heads held high on top of their curving necks. Even the camels were decked with large tassels and fine blankets. Some had draped over their shoulders the leather throws so typical of the Tuareg: turquoise green, earthen red, mustard yellow, and geometrical shapes dotted with beads and sequins. Along the bottom, the leather was cut in thin strips to make a fringe. The men strutted the camels back and forth near the group of singing women. This was a way for the men to show off their beautiful finery and how well trained their camels were. Go'at was riding Anarani, although they were not as bedecked as the others; such luxurious items had not been practical to bring along on this journey. Laila was delighted to see how gallant they looked together, regardless of what they wore.

The festivities were in full swing, and that meant that it was time for the camel race. There were six competitors. Those with the leather throws removed them; their heaviness weighed down the camels. As the women continued to drum and sing, the men trotted their camels to a distance which made them look quite small on the horizon. Just beyond was a wide valley between the rise of hills. One of the men walked with them to provide the starting call.

Typically, once the camels are positioned at the starting area, the race begins. But the group did not take off, milling around for quite some time. The women began casting puzzled looks, but they kept the music going. They were wondering what was delaying the men when, suddenly, they heard the shout that starts the race.

The women stopped singing. All eyes were on the dots headed their way. It was exciting to finally see each of the riders and their camels distinctly come into view. But it came as a complete surprise that the six racers somehow had turned into seven. Everyone shouted and yelped with excitement. The men were spread over a wide area, with two clearly in the lead. Laila was thrilled to see that one pair was Go'at and Anarani. They were just behind the winning pair by a head. Laila cheered for Anarani; he was making such strides. But the first camel found a spurt of energy that propelled him forward over the finish line, marked by the span between two men standing opposite each other.

As all the men and camels finished the race, the mystery of the seventh pair was solved. The seventh racer was Fatima's husband. The women were excitedly telling her what she already knew; Fatima had already spied him from a distance. Her heart leaped with joy! She ran toward him as he deftly slid off his camel in mid-stride. They came together, hugging Jack between them. The men knew he was going to surprise Fatima by coming to the *tende*. He was timing his arrival around the camel race. He had ridden from Tamanrasset and kept out of sight. Her husband had been unloading his pack in the valley just beyond, and had thus delayed the race.

Laila went over to Go'at and Anarani to congratulate their second-place win. She gave Go'at a hug. Anarani nudged her head and she turned to wrap her arms around his neck. She exclaimed, "How fast you are! You really showed up those other camels!" Anarani shook his head and gave her a wink. Laila was dying to talk with him, but knew it would have to be later, away from the crowd. She gave him another hug. Go'at gave her a wink and then led Anarani away so he could remove the saddle and give him some treats for his amazing performance. He was no young camel to have finished the race as he did.

## THE NAMING CEREMONY

The excitement of the race subsided and the camels were unsaddled. The *tende* was over and it was time to gather for the formal naming ceremony in the village. Everyone slowly walked, laughing and talking, back to the village. The men who rode in the race were playfully slapping each other on their backs with hearty congratulations, especially for the youngest participant who had raced for the first time. The men whooped and hollered around him with kudos for his good performance. Staying on a running camel is a skill that takes practice to master.

The fire was large in order to accommodate everyone. Fatima, her husband, and Jack, along with Amadou, Dassine, and Hamidou sat together. They motioned to Laila to join them. She made her way over with anticipation and trepidation. It was time to bring before the village a request she could not help but make. For the past two days she had done a lot of preparation for this moment, and now the time had come.

※ ※ ※

A few days earlier Laila had learned, while helping out in the birthing tent with Dassine and Fatima, what would take place during the naming ceremony. Fatima said that a ram would be sacrificed while proclaiming the baby's formal name. With the mention of killing an animal, Laila became quiet and stared out through the opening of the tent. Dassine and Fatima looked at each other, sensing the shift of her demeanor.

"Laila, what are you thinking?" Dassine asked.

Laila drew in a breath. "I don't know. But the moment you said a ram would be sacrificed, it felt like my father's presence came to me very strongly." She closed her eyes. In the background, Jack's small whimpers seemed to echo a little voice deep within that was trying to get her attention. After a few moments, she opened her eyes and said, "Fatima, Dassine. I feel there's something I need to ask you."

They turned to look at each other and then back at Laila saying, "What is it?"

She sat up and spoke. "Does a ram have to be sacrificed? I mean, hasn't there already been a sacrifice that is inherent in my father's name?" She paused to gather her thoughts, then continued.

"My father's love of the Sahara and its people grew deep and strong within him. During my journey here, along with what I learned from Amadou and Hamidou, I feel his life may have been sacrificed during the revolution for reasons that will never be completely understood. What I am wondering is, in honor of his death and his deep love of this culture, can his sacrifice represent and replace sacrificing a ram?" Laila wasn't sure where all of this was coming from. "And he loved animals too…"

Dassine and Fatima looked at each other again. A smile gradually appeared on Fatima's face, which seemed to float over and inspire Dassine's lips. Shifting Jack a bit to get more comfortable, Fatima responded to Laila's request.

"While my family and I follow the traditions of our ancient culture, we are also of the modern times. I go through these ceremonies because I want to preserve our rich customs. However, I am not, as you might say, 'wedded' to them. Instead, I do them out of respect for the elders, but I do not believe any harm will come should we not perform particular parts of the ceremonies. Mother, do you agree?"

Dassine responded, "Laila, we are honoring your father by using his name. What you are asking is out of respect for the sacrifice that he made. We may follow these customs, but I feel your request is one to be considered. My advice is that you talk to Amadou and Hamidou. Their wisdom will guide you in how to bring your wish to the community."

So advised, Laila sought out Amadou and Hamidou and asked if they would have time to talk with her. They asked that she return later in the day, which she did. Sitting in Amadou's tent, Laila presented her thoughts and the conversation she had with Fatima and Dassine. Amadou and Hamidou took in her words. They sat quietly for a moment, then looked at each other. Amadou spoke. "Laila, you bring an interesting request, one that we would like to discuss with each other as well as with those who are part of the ceremony. When we have made our decision, we will invite you to come back to finish this discussion." Laila bowed her head and left the tent.

## LAILA'S JOURNAL ENTRY

I left Amadou's tent today feeling a bit out of synch after

asking that a ram not be sacrificed during the naming ceremony. The question came to me: Was I being too righteous and intolerant to ask that part of an ancient, traditional ceremony be removed? Who am I that I should have even made the request? With this thought weighing on me, I turned around to go back to Amadou's tent to rescind my request. But as I took a few steps, I stopped. I stilled my mind to see if there was any other voice inside. And there was. It whispered, "Ask for what you want."

Out of respect for my father and his deep connection with these people, I humbly made a request. I know their answer will also be out of the same respect and connection. I will accept whatever decision they come to. With that in mind, I came back to Ami's tent to be alone and to write in my journal.

## LAILA'S SACRIFICE

"Laila! Laila!" Dassine was calling her name. She had fallen asleep after writing in her journal. Laila called out, "Here I am!" She emerged from the tent, smiling and rearranging her tunic.

Dassine walked toward her saying, "Ahh, yes, there you are. Amadou and Hamidou are ready with their decision. I am here to take you to Amadou's tent." Laila picked up her sandals, sitting just outside the opening, and strapped them on. Dassine linked her arm with Laila's as they walked. Laila felt reassured by Dassine's closeness, which relaxed her slightly nervous energy approaching the tent. Dassine left, giving her a big smile.

Sitting before Amadou and Hamidou, Laila tried to read their faces, but she saw no more than their usual stoic expressions. Hamidou broke the silence. "Laila, you have been walking the darkness you felt in your heart for many years. And surely Allah was most kind and merciful to have brought you here. Returning to this village where your father died was very brave of you. It took courage and strength. By taking this journey, both inner and outer, you are healing your heart. You are truly transforming your grief. Your capacity to love is expanding not only within you, but through all whose hearts are connected to yours."

Amadou continued, "The love your father shared still beats within our hearts. His sacrifice was ours as well, and so what you ask is not unreasonable. However, if the ceremony does not involve the slaughter of a ram, there will need to be some other form of sacrifice as a representation in its place. That, Laila, we leave to you to figure out. We have complete faith that you possess all that you need to work with this. Should you need to discuss anything, we are here to provide assistance. May Allah be with you, *Bishmillah*." With that, they bowed their heads to her indicating that the discussion was over.

Laila felt both relieved and nervous about their decision. On the one hand, she got what she asked for. On the other, it required coming up with a different type of sacrifice. Of what, she had no idea. So to think upon this, she headed out beyond the village for a walk. She sought the desert's emptiness as her companion, to help her process what was coming up from within as well as what she'd just heard from Amadou and Hamidou. She also secretly hoped to find her four-legged companion. She felt that Anarani's wisdom would help her understand how to carry out what she was asked to do.

It didn't take long before she saw Anarani coming from an area with scattered vegetation. Laila hadn't consciously chosen to go in that direction; but when she saw him approaching, she felt some subconscious part of her had guided her straight to him.

"Anarani!" Laila laughed. As they neared one another, he lowered his head and she gave his neck a heartfelt squeeze. "I have missed you very much, my dear friend! How are you?"

"A bit bored. But I have heard that soon a race will be held and I believe Go'at plans for us to run in it. As many days as I have been resting, I know I will show off how fast I am."

"I will be rooting for you, of course!" said Laila. They continued to walk.

"And you, Laila? What have you been doing in the village?" he asked her.

"Well, lots of help with the baby and preparing food for the naming ceremony. I feel very honored to be a part of what's happening. And..." her voice trailed off because she was still formulating how to tell him about her earlier exchanges.

"Yes?" They had reached an acacia tree and Laila sat down, which prompted Anarani to do the same.

Laila felt a bit awkward talking about animal sacrifice with an animal, even though it was not about killing. She knew that camels were eaten in the desert as well. She decided to be as forthright as he would be and just tell him her tale. He listened, chewing his cud as usual. When she ended with having to figure out her version of a sacrifice, he stopped chewing his cud for several seconds then asked, "Do you know what you will sacrifice?"

"Well, I took this walk to think about it and then I ran into you. So—no, not yet."

"From what I understand about this "sacrifice," it must represent something meaningful. Is that right?"

"Yes, giving up a life or something that is hard to let go of."

"Then the question must be, what is something that would be hard for you to let go of and how would you let it go?"

Laila loved Anarani's simple and to-the-point manner. This was exactly the question she needed to help her decide what to sacrifice in the name of Jack. They sat in silence, she and her beloved camel. As she contemplated his question, Laila looked down at her two *gris gris*—the one her father gave her and the new one that contained her blessing. Lifting up her father's, she suddenly felt her stomach sink as she said aloud, "Anarani, I think I can answer your questions."

◈◆◈

At the naming ceremony, the fire crackled. Everyone was silent, waiting. Amadou stood up to address the community. Laila was relieved when Hamidou leaned over to whisper that he would be translating Amadou's words.

"Today we welcome my grandson into our community by giving him his name in honor of Allah's most merciful presence." Fatima handed Jack to her father. The baby had just finished breastfeeding, and was sleepy. Amadou took him into his arms and gently lifted the small bundle, saying, "I hereby pronounce his Islamic name to be 'Sabur'. Let his name be a reminder that patience is needed to study the Koran, as well as to walk a life dedicated to Allah." Amadou handed the baby to Fatima. Jack's slight protest and squirming soon settled into sleep.

Amadou continued, "Over the past week, we have also welcomed Laila into our community along with the memories of her father, who tragically lost his life in this village. He was a dear friend. As you know, his name, "Jack," has been gifted to my grandson. *Inshallah*, these two arrivals were no coincidence. That is why I have spoken to all of you about breaking our tradition of slaughtering a ram as part of this ceremony. Laila requested that her father's sacrifice be honored instead." He looked over at her and nodded.

Hamidou finished his translation. She thanked him, then looked at Amadou and returned his nod. She took a moment to survey her audience. Their eyes were on her. The initial trepidation surprisingly disappeared. It was finally the moment to speak what she had been working on over the past two days, along with the help of the elders sitting with her. She had written down the words she wanted to say. But, taking a deep breath, she trusted that being in this moment was enough to speak what her heart had already written. Laila stood up and moved nearer the fire. Amadou served as her translator.

She began, "Loss is part of being. Being is living through loss. I have been living through the loss of my father who died twenty years ago in this village. Despite my sadness, fears, and loneliness, I followed my broken heart back to the Sahara and to all of you. It has been a journey of many years, and many miles. In these weeks as I journeyed here, I have learned much about life's struggles and longings—my own and those of the Tuareg. I learned how much my father opened his heart and felt your struggles, too. His death represents not only the tragedy of your revolution twenty years ago, but how that unrest continues to this day. Our hearts ache over and over when one culture forces their prejudice and power on another. My father could not tolerate this treatment, which may have led him into a dangerous position.

"The significance of his death runs deep within all of our hearts. My father's life has already been sacrificed. In honor of his name being passed on to baby Jack, I ask that we offer a substitute for the tradition of a sacrificial ram. I offer this *gris gris*, a gift from my father when I was a child. It holds the blessing that Amadou made."

As Laila pulled her father's *gris gris* over her head, Amadou began chanting the Koranic verse that it held: "Whether you conceal what is in your hearts or declare it, Allah knows it. Allah knows what is in the heavens and in the earth and he has power over everything." (Surah Al-i'Imran 3:29). She held it in her hand, gazing at its simple, rustic design. Smiling, with tears in the corner of her eyes, she lowered her hand toward the flames. She let the fire consume the material that held the blessing, while still holding on to the yarn necklace. When the blessing had burned, she released her grip on the yarn. In an instant, it was transformed into ashes and smoke, and carried off by the wind.

Once Amadou had finished chanting, Laila looked up. She said, "I learned from a very wise being about sharing vibrations and messages from the heart. The more we open our hearts to each other, the more it allows us to see, feel, and hear one another." She looked around the fire at all the eyes upon her. "And in so doing, it builds the strength of communities. Let this sacrifice be a symbol: One heart opens another heart. And by connecting our hearts, life is worth living."

Laila sat down.

The silence was broken moments later when Fatima handed her baby to Laila as she pronounced his name to the community, "Sabur Jack!" With that, the women ululated and shifted the energy into that of joy and celebration. The merriment continued with feasting, drumming, singing, and dancing until the wee hours of the morning.

At one point, Laila saw Anarani observing the festivities just on the edge of the fire's glow. She gathered some dates and made her way to him. He slurped up the treats she offered from her palms. She loved feeling his large, soft muzzle and warm breath. They walked in silence to be out of earshot.

"How are you after making your sacrifice, Laila?" Anarani asked.

"Anarani, there is no other word I can think of now than 'grateful'. I couldn't have done it without this community of people, or without you. It has all been an incredibly healing experience. I felt so alone for many years. And it has taken coming to the largest and emptiest desert in the world to finally feel my heart connected. It is through these connections that I have found a safe haven within my own heart."

"You will go back to your home soon," he said quietly.

"Yes, I must return home to let all that I have learned here sink in. I must allow the magic to work on me and to see what it calls me to do. I guess it's like when the *djinn* came to you and you had to learn how to use your gift to talk."

"I—" Anarani hesitated. "I will miss you, Little Laila."

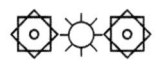

# RITE OF PASSAGE: STAGE III

# INCORPORATION

(Bringing new vision, insights, and knowledge
back to the community)

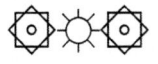

# A HEARTFELT DEPARTURE

On the morning that Laila, Go'at, and the men were leaving, the energy of the village was slower and measured. When Laila emerged from Ami's tent, she noticed that the children were focused on her from a distance. Their expressions held sadness. After she brought her backpack out for Baggee to carry to the camel loading area, she went over to the group and sat down. They approached her with hesitation, but she reached out to tickle some of them. One giggled, then another, and they fell into the familiar squiggling, tumbling puppy pile. She was going to miss all this playful interaction, but she was also looking forward to finally having a bathroom, a bath, a bed, and the comforts of modern living.

Gathering herself up from the children, she gave each one a big hug and another peace crane from her pocket. She had folded more as parting gifts. They followed her to where Go'at, Baggee, Ibrahim, and Ouhetta were assembled with the camels. As a matter of fact, the entire village was assembled to see Laila off. She gave each person a hug, saying *"Tenemert."* When she came to Dassine, Amadou, Hamidou, Fatima, her husband, and baby Jack, her emotions spilled over. This was not like how she and her mother had left so many years ago—in a rush and in deep pain. Now she would carry this web of connection no matter where she went. But it wasn't just from being here at this moment in time. She realized her heart had been entwined with this community since she was a child. Although she lived her life in a distant location, the seed that had been planted from her experiences growing up with the Tuareg kept growing in her heart. Her father's energy surrounded her here, and was especially acute with baby Jack. Her heart was brimming over in fullness.

Laila had another item in her pocket. This was a special gift she wanted to give Jack. "Fatima, I have something that was a gift to my father when I was born and I want to give it to Jack." She pulled out the silver cup she had decided to pack at the last minute before leaving the States. "This cup was made by Hamidou. I cherish it and I want Jack to have it now." Laila placed it in Fatima's hand and they hugged with Jack bundled between them.

"I will miss you, my soul sister," Fatima wiped the tears from her eyes. "And I have something for you." She opened her hand.

Lying on her palm was a stone in the most perfect heart shape. "I found this when I was a child. It has been one of my prized possessions. I want you to have it. May you always find love wherever you go, and whatever you do." They hugged again. This time really was "goodbye" or, hopefully, only "so long for now."

The caravan took its leave, illuminated by the glow of the rising sun, while the village stood watch. Laila kept looking back until their forms finally floated over and then disappeared into the horizon. Today, she did not mount Anarani. It was a day to feel the earth beneath her feet and to feel his huge, protective presence beside her.

✦✧✦

The day was almost at an end, but Go'at kept the pace going longer than usual. They didn't stop to camp until just after the sun went down. Although he had replenished the supply of food by asking Amadou and Hamidou to bring back items from the oasis, he knew it was better to aim for as fast a return as they could manage. Everyone was tired, so their evening's tasks were mostly performed in silence.

Sitting around the small glow of the fire, Laila noticed how the surrounding darkness cloaked the group and made them feel contained. At the same time, when she looked up at the sky, there was also the feeling of floating in the vastness of the universe. So few places on earth afforded an environment untouched by man's influence—the thick blanket of stars was unobstructed, making the heavens feel even closer. Everything feels magnified in the desert, for the desert teaches by taking away. And in that way, less was truly more.

## TIN HINAN, QUEEN OF THE AHAGGAR

"I, Tin Hinan, am of restless heart and soul. Looking out upon the comfortable confines of my beloved Tifilalt oasis, I long to see what lies beyond the beautiful, lush scenery that feeds my lips sweet dates from sandy soil. No longer is this enough to feed my soul. With a fierce nature in my heart, spurred on by the boredom of comfort, I ache to escape. And so on this night, I slip into the full moon night on my milk-white camel along with my faithful handmaiden, Takamet."

## SHARING THE TREASURED ELIXIR

Go'at had a going away present for Laila. It was a present only a Tuareg of the Ahaggar Mountains could give: to show her the monumental tomb of Tin Hinan, the legendary 4th century matriarch of the Tuareg. She was given the title Tamenukalt. It meant queen or leader, as well as "Mother of Us All." Her name translates to "She of the Tents." Go'at would take a route back to Tamanrasset that went by the tomb. The men kept it a secret so they could surprise Laila.

Toward the end of the next day, they made their way through flat sand and large clumps of scraggly, green grass and shrubs surrounding a mound of rubble. Curious, Laila guided Anarani over to Go'at's camel and asked him what it was.

"This," said Go'at as he pointed toward the mound of sand, rocks, and bricks, "is the tomb of Tin Hinan, legendary queen of our people. And it is where we will stay the night."

Ouhetta took the lead rope from Laila to couch Anarani. She and Go'at walked to the tomb and circled its large perimeter, composed of stones along with disintegrating bricks strewn over the ground - a testament to their former structure as a wall. Go'at put his arm out indicating a place where they could sit down.

"I will tell you of a legend about a noble woman who came from an oasis that is now part of Morocco. Her name was Tin Hinan. She and her servant, Takamet, left the Tifilalt oasis in the fourth century, never to return. Along the way, she bravely united the Tuareg tribes and established her kingdom here in Abalessa. We are descendants of a matriarchal lineage, saying that the warrior caste is descended from Tin Hinan and the peasant caste from Takamet.

"Laila, I wanted to bring you here as a last gift from the Sahara. Much like Tin Hinan, you left the comfort of your home to journey a long way. Although you will be returning, you will never return to being the person you once were. You have found treasures that this world has offered you. These treasures must be shared with your world. In the desert, the treasure that we must share lest we die is the elixir of water. Without water, there is no life. As we say, '*aman iman*', or, water is life." Go'at pulled out a pendant with a small glass teardrop charm. "This teardrop contains water from the Sahara. Let it be a reminder that your journey, like

Tin Hinan's, can be one of creating unity by communicating the elixirs of what you have learned. Only through sharing can there be meaning from your experiences." He offered her the necklace. Laila reached out and he gently placed it in her hand, folding his hands over it.

Go'at then continued. "The elixir of water also reminds us of our connection to the earth. Modern living is separating us from the sources that feed us. This dilemma is even affecting us in the desert as more young people leave the villages and move into the cities. It is getting harder and harder for those of us who grew up learning the ways of the desert to pass on this knowledge. We are competing with the material desires of belongings and money. Such desires go directly against nomadic nature." They sat quietly while the darkness cast the mound into a looming shadow. A slightly glowing aura surrounded it from the fire that the men had made on the opposite side.

Laila broke the silence. "Go'at, I can't express how grateful I am for all you have done for me. Your wise words, along with your guidance through the desert, are gifts I will treasure. I can't thank you enough. Thinking over all I have been through, it feels like a lifetime since I arrived. And I'm sure it will take time to process all of my experiences. I hope I can remember all that I have gone through so that I am able to share it with others."

"Ahh, but remembering every detail is not as important as letting the experiences flow through you," Go'at responded. "They will present themselves if you calm your mind and trust that they have permeated every cell of your being. When we go through life-altering experiences, especially those we've sought out, the impact necessarily shifts our energy. And, like Tin Hinan, we can rise to the challenges in a way that benefits more than just ourselves."

## LAILA'S JOURNAL ENTRY

Last night, I had a dream.

I am riding Anarani. We pass an unusually large, green, leafy bush and it seems to have a hole in the middle of the foliage. I am curious about what I see, so I dismount and go back. I approach it from the side and when I step around to see the hole, it's in the shape of a heart! The dense, oval bush surrounds a heart space that is filled by the blue sky. Spindly branches are growing into the heart, but I can see through it. Then the blue turns to a sparkling, star-filled sky and I am drawn through the heart. From this vantage point, I see that the stars are not just points of individual light, but that they radiate along threads that are all interconnected. I realize that I am suspended in an infinite webby soup that feels both heavy as a boulder and light as a grain of sand. I fit somewhere in between. It brings to mind one of my favorite words I learned in a college biology class: interstitial. "Living around, among, and between."

I woke up feeling my heart pumping in my chest—not from fear, but exhilaration. The transformation has taken place, or should I say is taking place...? For when there is transformation life truly begins. And it feels somewhere between being heavy as a boulder and light as a grain of sand, between fear and exhilaration.

## ROOTED, BELONGING, AND VASTNESS

That morning, Laila asked Go'at if she and Anarani could walk enough paces behind the group so that they could see them but also be able to talk without being heard. He gave the okay and let her know that when he waved his hand that would be the signal that she should start to follow. As they made their way onward, Laila saw that they were nestled in some of the most mountainous terrain of the Ahaggar. And at the same time there were still huge sweeping spaces in between. This made for spectacular scenery. As Laila and Anarani crested a dune, she gasped. Her eyes widened from their morning haze. Anarani stopped in response.

"Laila?" he asked.

"I'm okay. It's just that this view is the most breathtaking I have ever seen."

She slid off his back and they gazed out. The day's dawning light spilled over the ancient, untouched desert-scape. Laila and her trusted companion watched the birth of a new day. The rest of the group had gotten to the bottom of the dune, and were dwarfed by the expanse of space and huge massifs.

"Anarani, this is as pure as it gets. We are witnessing a part of the earth that has felt little to no interruption or influence by man for hundreds of thousands of years."

She leaned into to Anarani's tall, strong body contemplating this scene and this moment. Here was the clarity that she had been seeking. On this journey, she dared to walk to the threshold of her dark heart not knowing if the void would swallow her up. When she finally let go of her fears, it allowed her to not only find the universal beauty of this magnificent place, but the reflection of that universal beauty within herself. She hadn't felt such contentment in a long time, and she found it in a place far from her usual walk of life. It was like arriving home both within and without.

Laila loved the singular and clustered formations of the Ahaggar Mountains. There was no questioning their belonging, and in similar fashion she was sinking into that sense of her own belonging. Contentment is about such attachment, a feeling of inclusion. She was finally experiencing the rocky sturdiness of just being. From this perspective, the huge, denuded rock statues looked like chess pieces scattered over the endless horizon. Laila felt herself to be antlike in proportion to the grandness of the earth below, the vastness of blue sky above, and the wind filling the space between. All of these forces together produced that gasp in awe of standing in a universe, a galaxy, where this place and this definitive moment were only a blip on its infinitesimal scale. In the vastness of the Sahara Desert, Laila had never felt so rooted in her soul and in her life.

"The mystery of being is a permanent mystery."

*John Updike*

# EPILOGUE

Laila finished reading the final passage of her book, and the audience paused for several seconds as the images and words gradually drifted away into a shimmering mirage in their minds. They began clapping. She looked over at her mother who was in the front row of chairs in the bookstore. Katherine had tears in her eyes and, as much as Laila didn't want to cry, she also felt the tears welling up. Next to her mother, there was a beautiful woman wearing flowing robes who held a young boy in her lap. He was being very patient for his age. Fatima beamed at Laila.

"Thank you," Laila said as the clapping died down. "Now I would like to introduce you my mother, Katherine." The audience clapped. Laila came around the podium to encourage her to stand up. They hugged. Katherine turned, shyly waving her hand. "And this is Fatima with her son, Sabur Jack." Fatima stood up as the audience applauded them. They also hugged. Laila continued, "I only wish I could have the entire desert community, from Go'at and the men of the caravan, to Anarani, to Amadou, Dassine, and Hamidou here for you to meet in person. And, well, Anarani may not exactly be a talking camel," the audience chuckled, "but he is a very expressive one. Thank you so much for your interest in how they all inspired me, and for being here tonight." The woman from the bookstore let the audience know that Laila would be at the table to sign her book and answer any questions.

As the people moved about, Katherine took Laila's hands in hers and said, "Laila, that was beautiful. I'm so proud of you!"

"Thanks, Mom." She gave Katherine another hug.

"I wish your father could have been here, but maybe he is…" They smiled through their tears. Fatima was tending to Jack. He showed great curiosity about the people, as they came over to talk to him. Laila was ushered over to the table to sign her book, receiving congratulations along the way. She never thought a time like this would come—to share her life experiences in a way that would reach out to such a wide community, connecting so many hearts.

# THE RHYTHM OF THE SOUL

"The way through the desert is not a detour.
Who has not suffered emptiness, cannot deal with fullness;
Who has never lost the way, cannot value the signpost."

*Friedrich Schwanecke*

# DISCLAIMER

Although I have woven my fictional story in with anthropological and historical details about the Tuareg and the Sahara Desert of Algeria, I am in no way an expert on these topics. I gleaned much of my information from reading many books over the years, watching documentaries, as well as researching internet sources. I tried to ensure that what I found were authentic depictions and could be corroborated as facts. I also utilized what the Tuareg men on the vision quests shared with our groups during our time together. Their tales were told in a way that sank into my psyche.

In utilizing quotes from the Koran, I hopefully did so with care and respect. I am not a scholar of Islam. My apologies for any use or interpretation that is not based in that religion. However, I based the divination described in this story on what I experienced with our medicine man, Jumbo, on my 2005 vision quest.

## ABOUT THE AUTHOR

Lisa Diane McCall has a BS in Zoology and an MHS in International Health. She has worked as a public health professional for 25 years with services and research related to HIV/AIDS. For over a decade, she has been the director of the ALIVE (AIDS Linked to the Intravenous Experience) Study, an epidemiological study of HIV and HCV infection in people who have a history of injecting drugs in Baltimore City. The study is conducted at the Johns Hopkins Bloomberg School of Public Health and has reached its 30th year.

Lisa is a Certified Life Coach with an active practice.

This is her first novel, and so she is also a writer!